Yelena Dubrovina

PORTRAIT
IN AN OVAL FRAME

A novel

CHARLES SCHLACKS, PUBLISHER
Idyllwild, California, USA
2016

Yelena Dubrovina
Portrait in an Oval Frame
A novel

ISBN #: 1-884445-81-0

Printed in the United States of America

Charles Schlacks, Publisher
P.O. Box 1256
Idyllwild, CA 92549
USA
Schlacks.slavic@greencafe.com

Drawings by Helen Krasnoshchekova

Portrait of Rita by Inna Lazarev

Cover design by Yelena Dubrovina

In memory of my parents

TABLE OF CONTENTS

Portrait of Rita

Chapter One
Diary

*T*he train was passing through some small and unfamiliar towns, disappearing into the void of the waning day. The autumn music was noisy, absurd and yet sad, intertwining with the doleful sounds of the moving train. The melody reminded him of a wistful violin; the sounds clung to each other as if trying to linger on this earth. Sunrays rushed about the sky, searching for a narrow hole to peep through the heavy clouds. The small towns were slowly aging. They stooped under the pressure of the hovering sky. Day was giving way to early autumn twilight.

He sat by the window, watching with sadness the fading colors of the autumn day and trying to recall his father's stories about his childhood, youth, and the small town where he was born. Every time the train sang its road song, reminiscent of Beethoven's music, the sounds of the autumn violin would fall silent, causing some distant memories to come alive. They were just colorful shreds that he could not glue together because some important parts were missing, those that he had never asked his father about or had simply forgotten.

And then he thought about his mother whom he had never known. He imagined the outline of her face on the **window** glass, the familiar and yet so very unfamiliar face of the woman who had given him the gift of life. The evening fog thickened and took away her image, leaving him with his own reflection. He felt distressed with some unexplainable premonition, as if something were about to happen. And yet, how could he know that this cold rainy day would change his life forever?

* * * * *

Early on the evening of the fifth of October, 2003, a Philadelphia-New York local train pulled into the station. It came to a complete halt, decelerating and producing a muffled, metallic clangor, interrupting the sounds of the autumn music. As soon as the doors opened, impatient passengers squeezed through the exit and then, pushing and bumping into each other in their haste, spilled onto the platform. A tall, strikingly handsome man, smartly dressed in a striped Armani suit with a starched white shirt and a blue tie, was the last one to leave the train. He paused for a minute irresolutely, meditating and deeply inhaling the damp air, and then with his rather resilient, boyish gait hurried to the exit. Obviously, nobody was waiting for him, and he did not expect anybody to be there to greet him.

He strolled leisurely along the platform, attracting attention by his conspicuous, immaculate appearance, dignified bearing and the way he carried his head proudly above the crowd. Although he was not particularly waiting for anybody, he looked around several times before he stopped and sank down heavily on the station's iron bench, as if he did not know what to do next and simply wanted to think and relax. The man placed his light raincoat and suitcase next to him on the bench and glanced over the crowd. For some time, he watched with amusement the bustle of the crowded station while his well-tanned face expressed deep curiosity about the city people racing purposefully back and forth. He enjoyed this aimless time immensely, observing the life seething around him when his eyes met those of a pudgy, middle-aged man dressed in an ill-fitting business suit.

The stranger stopped, examining him through his tinted glasses until his face showed some kind of astonishment. He was probably the kind of loquacious, friendly man, who simply out of curiosity would pester strangers with queer questions or would unexpectedly break in on a conversation.

"Sorry for intruding, but I hope I am not mistaken. Are you Alexander Gold, the famous artist? Your name leapt out at me today from the newspaper. Do you know that there is an article about you in the *New York Times* accompanied by your photograph? I recognized you right away."

The man pulled off his glasses and stared at Alex with profound admiration. His eyes warmed when he stretched out his hand for a friendly handshake. Perhaps the stranger was pleasantly moved by a sudden opportunity to meet such a famous man. Alex glanced suspiciously at the officious stranger but extended his hand smiling shyly at such an observant art lover.

"Yes, in fact, I am Alexander Gold. By the way, do you happen to have the newspaper? I have not seen it yet. I am curious, very curious. So, it came out today, exactly two days before the opening of my exhibition. Very well, very well."

The man, impressed by Alex's unruffled demeanor, hastily buried his face in a fat leather briefcase, rummaging in it for the newspaper.

"Here it is. You can keep it, I have already read the article," he proclaimed and with an awkward promptness gave Alex the newspaper.

The man was searching for something else to say. However, noticing that the artist didn't express any interest in continuing their conversation, he bowed and scraped before Alex as if trying to show him his deep respect.

"Good luck with the opening," wished the stranger and, ramming on his hat, rushed away.

Alex did not open the newspaper, but still clutching it in

his hand, got to his feet and made his way to the exit, hoping to catch a cab to his hotel. He managed to hustle through the growing evening crowd which slowly funneled outside the station and disappeared somewhere in the mist of the New York streets. Along with the flow of passengers, he too was eventually pushed into the street, but seeing that the line for a taxi coiled like a long snake, and the rush-hour homeward-bound crowd was too desperate, he hesitated for a moment and then, groaning with frustration, decided to walk.

The muggy evening promised to be dull, bereaving him of any expectations of spending a pleasant time in New York. The grey and damp twilight just moved into the city, sifting out over the earth through the peepholes of patchy clouds that raced hastily across the sky. The city was about to welter in haze. Windows glowed softly with smoky-red, shadowy colors, hardly visible through the dense fog. Their indistinct lights traveled along the streets from one building to another like small firebugs flying in dark woods. The city noise, the streets—they all drowned in the sticky, foggy air, and the cold shroud of rain. Twilight, petering out behind the clouds, spread its dark wings over the city and grumbled at its unfairly short life. Finally, obscurity swallowed the earth. Alex peered into the fog, but nothing could be seen beyond its veil, as if there was nothing behind and nothing ahead of him....

* * * * *

After a long stroll through the damp city, the hotel room looked quite pleasant. It was freshly painted with a large window overlooking Manhattan. Alex put his wet coat down on the bed and strode across the room to the window. Managing to open it, he let the air ooze inside. He hoped that the fresh air would help him to ease his lingering headache and perhaps even lift a bit his crestfallen mood. The impending night thievishly crawled into the room, absorbing all the objects. Finally, everything was drowned in darkness. Without turning on the light, Alex started unpacking his small suitcase and putting shirts in the bottom drawer of the desk. Unexpectedly, he stumbled across a small notebook pushed far to the back of the drawer. With unaccustomed curiosity, he pulled it out, put on his reading glasses and switched on the table lamp near the bed. The blurred yellow cone of light from the shaded dusty lamp fell on the pages.

The notebook did not have a cover and was speckled in a tremulous, lax handwriting. It looked like someone was in a hurry to finish one sentence in order to start on the next one. To his surprise, it was somebody's diary written in Italian. Alex spoke five languages fluently, and Italian happened to be one of them. He gingerly flipped the pages of the notebook. One line particularly caught his attention, and he was compelled to continue reading.

"What is my life for if ugly worms eat my soul and my brains? I see and feel them elsewhere. They are like people who rummage into your soul and use your brain eating it up. I live in a state of fear...but fear of what? I don't know. I am afraid of this powerful force...the fear, probably the fear of losing those I love. I live in a strange space surrounded by apathy and coldness. My paintings are in museums all over the world. But what would I say if anyone ever asked me what I felt when I put those dark colors and ugly faces, distorted with fear, onto my canvases? Am I at war with myself? I look inward and feel that my vagabond soul has left me. It flies into emptiness, nothingness; my feelings are frozen, and I am tired of striving against my fate. There is a fissure in my heart that drives me mad. The only person I can share my thoughts with is my dear friend—loneliness. How long should I continue smiling at people if all I dream about is to be left alone...in solitude with my work? I imagine that my life crashed when I had to say goodbye to her...so many years ago. Perhaps, once making a mistake, we live to regret it till the end of our miserable and lonely life...."

Alex felt chilled by these words. The man was tormented

11

by something, maybe he was even insane. *He is probably a very unhappy man, a loner, he might be after all a famous artist. But what is his name?* Alex soliloquized. He was lost in his thoughts when the importunate and sonorous buzz of the telephone interrupted his train of thought. He flinched from this unexpected trill and picked up the phone. The male voice on the other line was unfamiliar to him. It wobbled and sounded nervous as he searched for the right words.

"Pardon me, sir, I am so sorry to disturb you, but I need to know—I mean I need your help. The fact is that I left something in your room. Do you mind if I stop by for a minute just to look? Please, sir, allow me to stop by. I will not bother you. This is something personal, something very important to me." Then the voice choked and he lapsed into silence, waiting for a reply to his query.

A long, unpleasant pause hung in air before he repeated in a barely audible voice, "This is something very important to me. I do hope you wouldn't mind if I drop in for a minute." The man spoke with a slightly detectable accent. Alex closed the notebook, feeling suddenly guilty for reading somebody else's diary.

"Sure, you can stop by. I will be in my room for another ten perhaps…fifteen minutes. You are welcome to look." Alex spoke sluggishly, trying to make every word sound clear, as if he were afraid that the man on the other end of the wire would not be able to understand him.

"I will be there in fifteen minutes. I will have the cab return to the hotel. Please, sir, wait for me, I beg of you. My name is…." The man paused again and finally concluded, "However, it does not really matter. I'll be there shortly. Thank you, sir, thank you so much."

Alex hung up the phone and rushed to put the notebook back into the drawer. Then he lay on the bed thinking about this unusual turn of events.

Who could this man be? And what was his name? Why did he suddenly change his mind about giving me his name?

Chapter Two

The Encounter

*A*lex was not superstitious. He was a strong, relatively down-to-earth man, but today, since early morning when he got up to catch the train to New York, he felt that his heart was beating faster. His wife was still asleep, curled up on her right side, as always turning her back to him. Trying not to wake her, he tiptoed to the kitchen to prepare his morning coffee.

While having breakfast, he thought about his life which was sufficiently filled and relatively happy. However, he always sought refuge in his work. Alex was the kind of a man who was greedy for books and for life, enjoying art that expressed happiness through voluptuous and vivid colors. He loved people, who were picturesque and loud, with many ideas and plenty of energy because they made him feel strong and alive. He had many friends—some remained in his past, but most of the time though he carried all his past possessions with him into the present—all his friends and lovers. He could find time for every one of them—time consisted of small shreds of space, where he could accurately place all his relations collected over the years.

Alex used to receive about five hundred holiday greetings from his "past," "present" and even "future" friends. In response, he had always send postcards according to his list, always finding a warm word for every one of them. Often his cards would come back unopened, but he had still continued sending them without even making an attempt to find out who during the years had disappeared from his prolific life, or why.

Although Alex considered himself a man without any prejudices, he was open to the unpredictable effects of predestination. This sudden phone call to his hotel room puzzled him, and he impatiently waited to see the author of such an unusual diary.

His ruminations were interrupted by heavy footsteps in the corridor. His thoughts went back to the notebook when he heard an abrupt knock at the door, nervous and powerful.

Alex swung the door open, and in the gloom of the corridor he could only discern the silhouette of a tall man, emerging from obscurity.

"May I come in?" He had a deep, husky voice which was marked by a shortness of breath.

"Please, come in." Alex moved aside and let the man enter the room.

* * * * *

An eerie feeling of presentiment made Alex stand for a while speechless and confounded. There was something strangely familiar in the man's imposing appearance and even his posture. The first idea that flickered into his head was that he had met him somewhere before. The man however did not even glance at Alex but began feverishly surveying the room.

Alex turned on the light and approached the stranger, scrutinizing him with some interest. As he was thoroughly inspecting him, the man turned to Alex and their eyes met. Alex reeled back and froze for a minute, starring in astonishment at the man. Stunned, they gaped at each other in complete disbelief, as if both had been struck by lightning—they looked liked a carbon copy of each other. The resemblance between them was striking. The man had a beard and seemed a little bit younger than Alex. His green-blue eyes gave the impression of indifference, and his whole appearance was like that of a hermit. Alex felt that he was looking at himself in the mirror—but perhaps at his own image from some years ago.

"Who are you?" The words escaped Alex, who was unpleasantly annoyed by the presence of his own mirror image.

The man hesitated for a moment, still recovering from shock, and then answered haltingly with an oblique smile, "My name is Eduardo Goldano, and I am an artist. But... who are you?"

"My name is Alexander Gold, and I am also an artist."

"Well, actually," Mr. Goldano stumbled over his words, "it seems to me...that I do know your name. The day after tomorrow is the opening of your exhibition at the Museum of Modern Art. I read the article in today's newspaper and saw your photo. It struck me then—the resemblance—but I didn't linger on it. There are so many people who look alike. Don't you think so?" He spoke as if trying to brush off the unpleasant fact that a stranger across the room was sharing such an incredible resemblance to him. He deliberately changed the subject.

"Your art differs dramatically from mine. It is happy and colorful. You might be a happy man, Mr. Gold," Eduardo said with a great deal of obvious brusqueness as his eyes continued to search the room, apparently eager to find his object and get out of there as soon as possible.

The word "dramatically" somehow disturbed Alex. He always tried to avoid that word, using it only under the most extreme circumstances. Alex glared at Eduardo for some time, scrambling to remember if he had ever seen any of his work before...but in vain.

"Actually, your name sounds familiar to me too, but I can't recall having seen any of your paintings. How strange it is that we are both artists," Alex said, his voice still lin-

15

gering on every word. "I can hardly get over the fact that such encounters may happen when you least expect them. Did you notice that we look almost like twins?"

Eduardo stared back at him, puzzled. "Yes, I have already mentioned to you that I did notice the incredible resemblance in our appearances, and even our last names have the same root 'gold.' But how could we be related? I live in Italy, and I was born in Austria after the war. How old are you?"

"I was born in Russia during the war. Look," Alex interrupted himself, searching for the right words, "I have just arrived and, honestly, I'm starving."

At that, Alex suddenly had an idea. He turned sharply to Eduardo. "Would you like to join me for dinner so we can continue our conversation? You forgot your notebook in a lower drawer. I saw it there. Anyway, what do you think about having dinner together, perhaps downstairs?"

And without waiting for his response, Alex began to pull on his jacket.

"I am tired to the bone, and I was planning to leave New York today. By the way, I have already given up my room."

"So, I should imagine," Alex smirked, realizing that he now occupied that very same room.

Hesitating for a minute, Eduardo added, "You know, I have always had a certain penchant for solving mysteries. Our encounter seems to me like a portent of destiny." Moments passed before Eduardo continued, "But perhaps there is some significance to our encounter...or even some mysterious sign."

He bent over the drawer and pulled out the notebook. Alex listened to Eduardo very attentively.

"I hope you did not read it. Usually, I put down all my thoughts on paper whenever I feel like talking to a friend." Eduardo's faltering laugh made an unpleasant impression on Alex, but Eduardo had already moved to the door, inviting Alex to follow him.

And it was only then Alex paid close attention to the man's manner which seemed insolent, out of sync with his rather sloppy attire of old frayed jeans and a threadbare blue sweater. This observation, along with the passages from his diary, made Alex think that the man was probably in a state of despondency, and yet he had this scarcely tangible charm that only increased Alex' curiosity....

* * * * *

On the way to the restaurant, they rode the elevator in silence, scarcely finding words—each one was engrossed in his own thoughts. To their surprise, the restaurant was almost empty at the dinner hour. The subdued, misty lights of the chandeliers reflected in the mirrors, adding to the whole interior an eerie sensation of unreality. The walls were painted in a dark red color. Flickering candles were burning on every table, casting yellow, almost magical shadows around them. Instantly, such an enchanting setting created a delightful atmosphere of intimacy that disposed them to a heart-to-heart conversation.

They both noted the expression of bewilderment on the waiter's face when he ushered them to their table. The situation began to amuse both of them. They exchanged conspiratorial glances and smiled at each other. Somehow, to his own surprise, Alex began feeling a certain affinity with this stranger that he couldn't yet explain even to himself. His natural curiosity about people's lives made him start the conversation first.

"Well, Eduardo, how much time do you have in New York? When does your plane leave?"

Eduardo wagged his head. "When am I leaving?" He questioned himself pensively. "Hmm....I hope, soon. You probably realize—I have already missed my plane. Well, to tell you the truth, I have never liked New York anyway. Every time I visit this city, I am always flummoxed by its meaningless vanity. To me, it's just a faceless crowd where I feel so very lonely. The city colors look washed-out, as if they are bathed in dust or smoke, like today, for example. So, every time I am in New York, I have a desire to disappear, vanish—maybe because I prefer the clear colors of Rome to the washed-out colors of New-York or, let's say, perhaps clarity to uncertainty. Yes, yes, I always prefer clarity," he repeated, avoiding Alex' puzzled eyes and then explained, "In New York I feel somehow sinking into a cold solitude, drowning in its heavy mug. As an artist, I prefer the natural colors of nature. I am probably only an uncurious and selfish observer of an unintelligible and unfriendly throng of strangers in this city, foreign to me after all."

He mulled over something for a moment, as if choosing the right words. "Oh, yes, going back to your question. Does it really matter to you when I am leaving? Heaven knows, as I said, I have already missed my plane. I was on my way to the airport when I discovered that I had forgotten my notebook in the hotel room and phoned you."

The waiter brought them a menu and the drinks from the bar that they had ordered.

"Do you believe in destiny?" Alex continued his questioning.

Meanwhile, Eduardo finally relaxed and, settling comfortably in the chair, sipped his drink. "I probably missed the plane because I had a presentiment of today's meeting. As I said before, both our names have the same root—'gold'. We and our last names are congeners, and in addition to all these odd coincidences, we are both artists. I don't know about you, but I am actually greatly perplexed by these facts. In such a case, I should admit—I do really believe in destiny. What say you about it?"

He emptied his glass and flagged the waiter to bring another one. Alex took out a cigar case and lit his favorite Hawaiian cigar but did not touch his drink. Drawing slowly on his cigar, he was mulling over Eduardo's keen observation, still unable to express any emotion about such a coincidence.

However, he did feel an eerie aura of fascination about Eduardo.

Finally, Alex replied while inhaling a smoke from his strong cigar, "I have to agree with you. Of course, it's quite odd. Such things seldom happen indeed, but we might even be kin. Why do you think I invited you to have dinner with me? I am just as curious as you are."

Alex pushed a cigar case across the table, inviting Eduardo to join him in a smoke as he mused over his drink. Eduardo opened the case, then instantly changed his mind and pushed it back to Alex. He shook his head in denial.

"I used to be a heavy smoker, like you, but I gave up smoking some years ago. Perhaps, after I have learned from my mother about the fate of my father...." He abruptly stopped. "Anyway, I decided to get rid of such a temptation. I recommend that you do the same."

"I am afraid I don't have enough willpower to do so. I am following a piece of advice given by Oscar Wilde—to get rid of temptation, you have to yield to it." Alex burst out laughing.

Puffs of heavy smoke from the strong Hawaiian cigar rose above their heads, and Eduardo began coughing. Alex put the cigar down in the ashtray and leaned back in his chair. For a moment only, they were both deeply submerged in their own ruminations, when Alex reflected.

"It just occurred to me that we should both make an attempt to look into our past. Who knows, maybe we would be able to find some common roots, some crossroads."

"Sure enough, it might not be a bad idea at all. You could be right, maybe somewhere in the past our lifelines intersected? Let's try to dwell on our past. You should start first, Alex."

Eduardo leaned forward excitedly, and Alex registered a kind of childish interest in his penetrating, aquamarine eyes.

"In this regard, allow me to tell you a story about my parents and grandparents the way I heard it from my father

19

before he died. It might shed some light on the mystery we have encountered today. Remarkable or not, I hope this intricate narrative will be convincing enough...." He floundered for a moment and coughed, clearing his throat.

To the pleasure and surprise of both, their conversation began to take on a kind of hearty intimacy.

Alex continued, while Eduardo tried to maintain his customary equanimity, "I don't know if it has anything to do with you, but at least we should try to find any common roots if of course they exist. You have to be patient with me—my story will embrace two generations of my family history. I hope I will not bore you. So, looking back into my father's recollection, I have to say that I am amazed how different life is nowadays than it was then...."

Alex tasted his wine, anticipating the furtive pleasure of relating the history of his family that he had never told anybody before, including his own wife. Finally, taking out another cigar, he puffed on it several times and only then, sinking deeply into the chair, began his narration.

"Look, Eduardo, to be objective, and not to be too boring, I will try to tell my story in the third person. I'll start it from the day that changed forever the lives of our generation. So it goes....A hot and muggy summer day of June 22nd, 1941, was drawing to a close...."

Chapter Three
Remembering the Forgotten
The Beginning of War

A hot and muggy summer day of June 22nd, 1941, was drawing to a close. Mark and Leon rambled through the woods and along the banks of the river Emenka which meandered around their small provincial town called Nevel.

Nevel was an old town, first mentioned in Ivan the Terrible's will as among the towns that had been founded during his reign, probably before 1580. Jewish people had begun settling in Nevel since the middle of the 17th century. By the time of World War II, Jews made up half the town's population. Once a historical town with a diverse culture of old monuments, churches and synagogues, its face completely changed after the Russian Revolution. The only major church that survived demolition was the Holy Trinity Church, an old building of modest architecture, topped with a steeple and overlooking the astonishing beauty of Lake Nevel. Four streets branched out from the river, and coming together in the center of town, formed a small square named after Karl Marx. Many years ago, a monument to him had been erected in this central square to perpetuate his greatness. The monument was huge in size and seemed even more grandiose in comparison with the small buildings surrounding the old square of their town.

Mark and Leon, enjoying their summer vacation, spent their day away from home, going for a spin around the torturous river-course that disgorged into the Lake Nevel. Mark used to sit for hours by the river, contemplating the view he had always loved and watching the way the river quietly curved around its steep banks and sharp stones. As an artist, he felt a magical attraction to its shining, limpid waters that played with the colors of the falling day and approaching twilight.

They stopped at an effervescent brook to quench their thirst when a soaking rain and strong wind tore open the sky. Suddenly, the surface of the river began winking and plopping in the rain. It began moving faster, becoming darker and darker, as if foreseeing a disaster. And only the steady reflection of a lonely streetlamp in the river, disturbed by a strong, howling wind, moved along with the fast raging water. Mark and Leon took off their shoes and gingerly waded across the shallow part of the river, right before it flowed into the lake. Dusk began creeping upon the lake and the woods, brushing away the bright colors of the summer day.

"I am afraid that a bad storm is brewing." Leon announced as they reached the other side of the river.

Mark didn't reply right away and continued lagging behind Leon toward their house, which could already be seen perched on the cliff, in seclusion at the very turn of the river and near the picturesque lake. Beyond the house, the white roof of the local synagogue with its carved frilled eaves was visible from far-off. A small Jewish cemetery with a wooden fence, the main attraction for the local kids, was attached to the old synagogue.

"Please be quiet, Leon. I can hear silence exchanging words with the dragonflies, or, on the contrary, the dragonflies are trying to start a conversation with silence. Can't you hear it?"

"All I can hear is a fish sloshing about in the bottom of

the river," Leon replied.

Mark pressed a finger to his lips, making a sign to Leon to be quiet, but Leon didn't pay any attention to his brother's words. The wind caught the fine drops of rain, and through its mist he noticed a looming silhouette approaching them.

"I behold a ghost," laughed Leon, but his heart began to leap up with premonition.

A girl in a red dress ran toward them, waving and shouting something at the top of her lungs. At last, her words reached their ears: "The war, the war." It was all they could make out, overwhelmed with a sudden foreboding.

They hurried to Rebecca, their eldest sister. Only now, approaching her, they saw her face twisted with pain and fear. She slowed down, still puffing after running, and stretched out her hands as if seeking their support. Murmuring over and over again the same words, "the war, the war," she fell heavily into their arms.

"Rebecca, please stop crying. Tell us what has happened," Mark demanded, staring at her in disbelief while Leon tenderly stroked her messy hair.

Her shaking body reminded them of leaves shaking in the wind. And then, haltingly, still heavily breathing, she proceeded to tell them what had happened.

"You left at the crack of dawn to go to the lake; mother and I were about to leave the house to go to the food market, and father—to the synagogue when Igor appeared on the doorsteps—he looked so awful. 'Turn on the radio,' he shouted, 'Molotov has announced that early this morning without any warning the German Army crossed the border and advanced into Russian territory.' I have been looking for both of you all day long. What are we going to do now?"

Rebecca stopped crying and, looking questioningly at her brothers, continued, "We need to hurry up. Father is waiting for us. I heard that the Germans are not far from Vitebsk, and they may be here very soon. I am frightened. A real danger is hovering over our heads...."

* * * * *

"I am not sure yet why you are telling me about Nevel, but please continue."

Eduardo threw a quizzical glance at Alex, attempting to apprehend what he had just heard. Alex quashed a feeling of disappointment and tilted back in his chair, staring for some time pensively into space before he began talking again.

"How little we know now about the war. We show less and less interest in events related to our parents and grand-parents. But our past does not disappear—it comes back to haunt us, reflecting our present and our future. Tomorrow will not come without yesterday. No matter how hard we try to forget, to erase yesterday from our memory, hide it deep in our archives, it still lives in every cell of our brains, hearts and souls. What is happening today in the world has its roots in the past," he said reproachfully.

Eduardo nodded in agreement.

"But coming back to my story....Who would have thought that Germans would invade Russia? In 1939, shortly before the Second World War started, Stalin signed a non-aggression pact with Germany. It stated that the Nazis would not attack the Soviets, and the Soviets would do the same. Eight days after the pact had been proclaimed, Germany invaded Poland, and the Second World War began. Hitler believed that he would be able to defeat Poland quickly and hoped to complete the operation by late winter of 1941. As for the Russians, to win the war became a matter of life and death." He threw another glance at Eduardo, who listened to him with bated breath. "Anyway, I'll make my case, and it's up to you to connect the dots. Well, what was I saying before? Oh, yes...."

Alex gazed at Eduardo one more time, as if suddenly realizing something and then, collecting his thoughts, continued, "When they returned home, the whole family, including their mother, father and brother-in-law, were already sitting around the kitchen table...."

Chapter Four
Final Decision

*W*hen they returned home the whole family, including their mother, father and brother-in-law, were already sitting around the kitchen table. Who could know what was in their hearts? Were they horrified, afraid, stunned? No, none of those—they were rather shocked by the sudden development of events. The word "war" struck them as the utmost unreality, almost nonsense, something that they could have only read about in books or seen in movies, but now it had become so tangible, so real.

Perhaps only some old men in their town foresaw the evil days to come. But who would have believed them when the sky was blue and the sun was bright? They couldn't accept the fact that their happy and peaceful life was about to change or end. They had read before about World War I, but now it was happening, happening to them, and the Germans were not far from their very own town. Suddenly, white turned into black, light into darkness and known into unknown. The bright summer colors of life faded before their own eyes. What awaited them? What about their dreams of love or the future? Did they now have any future? In a whiff, these thoughts flashed through their minds. The time of awakening had now arrived. In one instant, their fate had become intertwined with the fate of their country, and they had to face it with courage. Nothing mattered anymore, nothing, except defeating the enemy and saving the lives of those they loved.

Their father, a rabbi at the local synagogue, who was regarded as one of the wisest and most respected man in their town, presided over the meeting. A single candle flickered in the middle of the table, throwing a dim light on their worried faces. Mark glimpsed at his father's face across the table, noticing the deep furrow between his brows as he began talking, carrying the news with the utmost fortitude.

"My children, I am afraid that we have dire days ahead of us. Our country is facing a great calamity. The German Army has invaded and attacked our country, and is now about to reach Vitebsk. How horrifying and how sorrowful it is. My heart tells me that we, the Jews, are in great danger. I believe that in times of trouble we should cling together. And now, I think that we should leave this town, all of us, before the Germans get here. However, I daresay that you, Igor, is hopefully safe, and yet you should go with us."

He leaned across the table, as if wanting to get a better look at his son-in-law, Rebecca's husband, a Russian man. He had been part of their family since his childhood when his parents were executed by the Bolsheviks. Igor blanched on hearing those words.

"Actually, I do think that we are all safe. I am sure…I thought…to some extent many people would like to join the German Army to escape the Soviet regime. Why do you think they would kill the Jews? It's nonsense. They didn't kill any Jews during the First World War. Why would they do it now? Suffice it to say that the Germans are people of great culture; they gave the world so many great names: Goethe, Heine, Nietzsche, Wagner…," he counted, stuttering and wallowing with his speech, "Rebecca should stay with me. I am here to protect her. I am almost ten years older than she. You are all cowards to run away. I do believe in German virtue and that the German soldiers are our liberators.

Trust me—"

He hadn't finished his sentence when Mark reared up and shot back deeply offended. "Trust you? Are you kidding me? God damn, Igor, what a foolish idea! What are you trying to pull on us—to live with the Nazis? Do you think we don't understand what communists have done to you, to us and to our country? Nevertheless, I am not going to abandon my motherland when she needs me the most. I am going to join the Red Army. What about you, Leon?" He turned to his twin brother.

"Sure, I'll go with you, Mark," Leon's voice muffled a bit as he covertly glanced at their mother.

The mother sat motionless, clinching her hands on her knees, thinking how much alike and yet different the twins were. In her late fifties, she was still very attractive and looked younger than her husband, who was nine years her junior. The mother surveyed the room with her sad eyes and then stared at the paintings which covered all the walls of their small house. Mark's watercolors had dramatic colors and disturbing emotions. He had a rare gift of penetrating into the secrets of nature. Leon's work was more abstract, a collage of wild colors and unrealized imagination. *How different the boys are,* she mulled again. *Mark—strong, but sensitive, almost like a girl, and Leon—weak, but determined, and yet both are so emotional.*

She was proud of their natural aptitude for art. *Damned war! Now, all their dreams would be shattered.* Mark had been studying medicine in Leningrad and was taking art courses while Leon's dream was to become an architect. All of a sudden, Rebecca's shaking voice sank into her consciousness.

"Please don't quarrel. We have no time for that. I have some really good news—Igor and I…we are going to have a baby. Surely all of you have already noticed that I am almost five months pregnant. You see, I can't leave now."

Probably any other day it would have sounded like a

thunderclap, but now....A dark silence reigned in the room for some minutes until their father raised his voice, "Congratulations, my children. This is great news. Mazel Tov.[1]" He turned to his wife as if looking for her support, and then continued, "Why didn't you tell us before? Do you think we are all blind? However, it's not time to argue now...."

Confused, Rebecca didn't utter a word. It was Igor's idea after all to keep it a secret from her parents.

"Well, you know, Rebecca," her father went on, looking her straight in the eyes, "I always opposed this marriage because you were raised together, almost like brother and sister, still you are a grown-up woman now, and your fate is in your own hands. At least, listen to your father and come with us; leave Nevel for the sake of your unborn child. Even being the wife of a Russian, you are still a Jew, and it is dangerous for you to stay here. Listen to me, Rebecca, I am more experienced and wiser than you are. I want my grandchild to be safe. As for you, boys, it breaks my heart to say goodbye to you."

He swallowed back tears and stroked his beard.

"But you made the right decision, and I understand the need to protect our country and our pride. I wish I could join you, but unfortunately my poor health will not allow me to do so."

On an impulse, Rebecca got up and approached her father. She wrapped her arms around him and put her head on his shoulder as she used to do in her childhood when she was about to cry.

"Dad, I truly think that it is too risky for you and mother to take a long trip to God knows where. Nevertheless, I suggest that you should pack and leave town immediately. You have to escape the Nazis and get as far away as possible. Please listen to me and do as I ask you. I beg of you because I love you. I promise—I'll be waiting here for your return.

---

[1] Yiddish for "god luck"

You have to understand—I can't leave Igor alone, and I can't really go very far in my condition. I will rely on God and entrust my fate to Him." She was so determined that it was folly even to persist in asking her to do otherwise.

The teakettle whistled on the stove, and the wind rattled loudly at the windows as they spoke late into the night, hashing over their plans and their actions. It was decided that Eliza and Samuel, their parents, should get to Kalinin and then take a boat. They would travel up the river Volga to Ufa, the capital of Bashkiria, where they had some distant relatives. Presumably, they would be out of danger there. They hoped that the German Army would not move far into the country. After hours of arguing, persuasion, changing plans and Rebecca's tears, a final plan was approved.

* * * * *

The shock of the disaster reverberated quickly throughout the region, and the whole town was now astir with this sinister news. In just one day Nevel had become unrecognizable—the streetlights had been turned off, and the warm, grey dusk enfolded the town. The main street and central square, usually crowded, were now deserted. The anxiety of separation, farewells, women's tears and the pallid faces of men had suddenly become their only reality. Their favorite old waltz, The Waves of Danube, had been chortled on the radio all day long. Its lingering music was heard everywhere, but now it sounded like a farewell hymn to their youth and their past. That hot summer night united the hearts of the citizens of Nevel in their sorrow, grief and uncertainty about the future.

The next day, some neighbors and relatives joined the rabbi for their final deliberation. Many of them still did not want to leave—they too, like Igor, believed in the virtue of the German nation, unable to perceive the extent of the great catastrophe awaiting all of them.

Again, late at night, they gathered around the kitchen

table contemplating, wrangling and discussing the latest news. They heard that Vitebsk was on fire, Polozk on fire, and the Germans were not far from Nevel. Impossible...it was impossible...only because they had believed that it could never happen to them. It was so hard to imagine that maybe tomorrow they would be dead, and their houses, their small, cozy dwellings, would be destroyed along with their happy lives. The heated debates had exhausted everyone. Women cried foreseeing their future; men were deeply occupied with their own ruminations.

O, Lord, how did you allow this to happen, why didn't you protect us? Bound by shared calamity, a woman asked the rabbi these questions, but even he, the wisest man in town, could not answer them. The uncertainty of tomorrow, the betrayal of their trust in God made it clear to their neighbors that the time had arrived to take their lives into their own hands.

The shadows of the night ominously blinked on the paintings and the white walls of the house, perched and isolated on the cliff at the very turn of the river and near the picturesque lake. The last ripples of thunder, like the remote sound of guns, were heard from far away, beyond the woods. The day of their parting barreled in faster that they had ever expected....

* * * * *

The night before their farewell Mark had a dream—a broad plain of snow sprawled before his feet. He stood in the middle of this totally white space, surrounded by white mountains. Everything around him was white: the sky, the moon, the earth and the air. He was completely dazzled by the pure whiteness of this ambient space and the splendor of the early December morning—clear, ethereal and cold. He could almost touch the air and feel it, feel how it was pressing heavily on his lonely figure, standing in the unfathomable open space, and it was only his body that threw a dark shadow on the snowy ground.

Unexpectedly, far beyond the horizon, he saw an indistinct light, and then...shadowy silhouettes....swimming out of the night towards him. For some time, he could even sense their presence, but then he realized—they were only shadows—the shadows of the dead. And at this very moment, there was no longer any boundary between the living and the dead. The ground began to shift under his feet, and he found himself floundering about in deep snow moving toward the shadows. His hands stretched out, trying to reach for them. Suddenly, among the moving dead, he saw his own ghostly reflection. The wind whipped up, the sky darkened, and the white turned into black: the earth, the moon, the air, the mountains and all the shadows became invisible. Their spirits were gone, lost forever somewhere in the universe.

His dream was like a short episode from a silent movie—black-and-white. The vision dissolved slowly in his consciousness, and he opened his eyes. He was awakened by a weird and unearthly rustle of the night. The room was still plunged into darkness, but a scarcely tangible feeling of spiritual presence and fear of death were still in the air. He raised his head from the pillow, dazzled by an eerie light coming through the open window. A lonely, resplendent star was shining above, from the unknown, the bright star—his celestial guide—which would always watch over him from another world and illuminate his path, no matter which way he might choose to go....

Chapter Five

The Invasion

*O*n the 15th of July, 1941, the German Army invaded Nevel. The whole horizon glowed with fire. Covered with heavy dust, the German tanks, cars and motorcycles rumbled along Vitebsk Avenue, wreaking havoc among the citizens of Nevel. Enemy warplanes, like ominous black birds with widespread wings circled the town scattering death into every corner of their peaceful country lives. The main square and usually noisy streets were completely deserted, as if fear and anxiety had turned them into black empty holes. Although the whole town was astir with news, people remained hidden in their homes, hoping for the best, even though anticipating the worst. The best never happened, and the old town froze suffocated with fear and horror. The invaders were on their way to plunder the town, shackle souls, enslave minds and break spirits of its citizens.

The women and children fearfully watched the invaders through the curtains on their windows. They saw the motionless faces of the German soldiers dressed in green uniforms, holding guns and ready to shoot their innocent victims. They had already heard about the Nazis' infernal cruelty, the burning houses, the thousands of graves, and the extermination of the Jewish population, including women and children.

Soon afterwards, the town itself was on fire. Some old

33

wooden houses, churches and synagogues were already ablaze, fiercely belching fire into the quiet summer sky. One by one, engulfed in flames, like toy-houses, many of them had collapsed. On the first day of the invasion the Nazis took prisoners—sixty members of the Soviet army—and carried out a bloody massacre in the backyard of house #58 on Vitebsk Avenue. Then they threw the dead bodies into a hole and covered them with mud. Some buildings spared by the fire had been immediately turned into prisons where the massacre continued every single day. Consumed by fear, during the first night of invasion people could not sleep. Drunken Germans soldiers sang their songs loudly, shouted, drank wine and beer, and launched rockets into the cloudless sky. The horrific period of German occupation had begun with the revelry of the Nazis, the hunger and fear of the local population. During the German invasion, from July 15th, 1941, until October 6th, 1943, over 7,000 Russian soldiers and 8,000 of Nevel's citizens were executed.

* * * * *

The 15th of July, turned out to be a fraught day for Rebecca. The nocturnal blackness had just hidden in the folds of the clouds, and the first shaft of sunlight filtered out through their heavy blanket and through the window chinks, dispersing its sheen all over the room. Rebecca rose up, not being able to stay in bed any longer. At dawn, when she stepped out of the house to bring some water from the well, she heard cars purr in the distance. And then a huge monstrous shadow swept across the sky and a strip of black haze floated above the town. Watching this flying black cloud, she realized that the dire days of war with all its destruction, grief and sorrow, were hiding behind this fast-moving shadow.

Every day now, had she struggled to quell a growing fear of death but in vain. She walked around the house, plunged deeply into thoughts, when her neighbor, an old Russian woman, swung past her.

34

"The Germans are coming," she announced jerkily on her way home, but her voice was drowned out in the roar of the warplanes.

Rebecca didn't hear her words but saw the woman's pallid face and her eyes full of horror. Meanwhile, her neighbors, swooning with fear, crept out of their houses. The street was deluged with old women and children. It hummed with their agitated voices.

"There are tanks moving along Vitebsk Avenue. I saw them with my own eyes," one woman was telling her story when a first lonely shotgun fired somewhere close to their street.

And as if horror had gripped them by the throat, they became silent. One by one, pushing their children in front of them, they quietly tiptoed to their houses. The rusted locks made mournful sounds, and the doors closed behind them. The shutters came down, separating their past from an unknown future. But Germans soldiers were already knocking at their doors demanding milk, water and food.

Rebecca, along with her neighbors, returned to the house and clung to the window. Clouds of heavy smoke hovered low above the cemetery, the lake and the river. The red sheen of flames wounded the sky. Usually a clear blue, it was now badly bleeding. The cascade of the dispersed sparks reminded her of holiday fireworks when, with her parents and her brothers, she watched the festivities from the banks of the river Emenka. For a brief moment, she had forgotten about the war, but then a first lonely shotgun blast rang out somewhere close to their street. Rebecca was clinging to the window, trying to see what was happening when her husband's voice intruded into her thoughts.

"Rebecca, Rebecca," Igor flew into the room, "they are here, our liberators, our future!"

With some difficulty Rebecca forced herself to return from her childhood memories. She didn't say a word to Igor, just turned away from the window and went to the kitchen to heat his lunch.

"Please go and wash your hands," she demanded entering the room. She put a bowl of soup on the table in front of him.

"You look pale. What's eating on you? I suppose it's not my fault that your brothers went to war. I could go too, but I have different plans. I want to live in a civilized society. I hate the Soviet regime that murdered my parents and other innocent people. You know all about it, and you hate them too."

"But it doesn't mean, Igor, that you have to betray your country, your friends, your relatives, even your wife...at the most difficult time of our lives. Who has created such a golem out of you, Igor?"

Uncontrollable anger surged up in him when he heard her brutal words. His face twisted in pain, and he arched his eyebrows in disbelieve—her words enraged him.

"Hang that all, including this country! Rubbish! I didn't betray our country—communists did. My parents were innocent, but they had to die for their allegiance to a cause. And you...don't ever dare to talk to me like that. Don't I take good care of you?"

He got up and in a fury smashed the dish. Soup spilled on the tablecloth, and its smell made Rebecca feel like vomiting. She had not eaten all day long, saving food for her husband.

"I can't take it any longer." He shot her another furious look.

"Scram, scram! I couldn't care less. Leave me alone," her words reached his ears despite her sobbing.

Slamming the door, Igor huffed out of the house and didn't come back until late at night, drunk. Rebecca sulked for a couple of days, but unable to bear her silence for too long, he soon approached Rebecca.

"I apologize, Rebecca, don't be mad at me," he rasped grudgingly, almost repentant, trying to reach for her hand.

She pulled away from him, still struggling to forgive him, though at this moment it didn't really matter to her anymore.

"I accept your apology, but you have changed, Igor. You are not the same person," she retorted flatly.

In order to avoid any further quarrels, she opened the door and slipped outside. She was glad that he didn't follow her.

That summer was generous with warm, cloudless and soft evenings, but the quiet was disturbing, as if misery and death hid behind every corner, every tree, behind the black tranquility of the night. Rebecca was scared. Now she sensed danger in every whiff of a soft breeze or crackle of a tree branch. And yet she longed for her usual long walks by the river or her morning bath in the translucent water of the lake. A pleasant confluence of peaceful scenery and unusual serenity among all those horrors made her just walk around the house for some time.

She couldn't remember how she reached her favorite secluded place. The transparent lake met her like a loyal lover, caressing her naked body with tender touches and adoring her unadorned beauty, fluorescent in the blue moonlight. She lay back on the mirrored surface of the lake, letting the water envelop her, reaching her chin and licking her face. She then swam for a long time until the tired moon bade her goodbye and turned into a tiny fireball, reminding her of the enemy warplane, as it flew away.

Rebecca threw her body on the warm grass, drifting slowly into a delirious slumber. The night was unusually quiet. She was cradled by the sky, and the stars sang to her their lullaby. Blurry images from the past of her parents, her brothers, schoolmates—all flooded her disturbed sleep.

She woke when the first pale sunrays showered their light on the grieving earth, cutting through the transparent waters of the lake and then drowning somewhere in its depth. She didn't know for how long she had been sleeping, but the mingled tumult of birds singing and the loud explosions somewhere near her made her rush home.

When Rebecca got back, Igor was still heavily asleep, and the smell of alcohol poisoned the air. She drew the curtain to create a nocturnal dimness, and exhausted, went to bed to continue her slumber.

Waking up late in the afternoon, Rebecca found the door wide open, and Igor already gone. She lazily stretched out and indulged in deep thoughts. She missed her parents, her brothers, her friends, and most off all their happy lives before the horror of war. She had no news from her parents since the day they had left but prayed everyday for their survival. Finally, she decided not to pay any attention to Igor's ignominious behavior but instead to concentrate on her own wellbeing and eagerly awaited baby.

Chapter Six
The Letter

*F*rom that day on everything went wrong. Most of the time Rebecca stayed home, reading or sewing clothes for her unborn baby. At night, she would sit by the window staring at the black surface of the river where it merged with the earth, forming one whole mass. The sky, the earth and the water—everything moved together, submerging into a world of de-lirium. Poor Rebecca, she still could not comprehend what was going to happen to all of them—her friends, her relatives, and those she loved the most. Her thoughts went back to her mother and the letter she had given to Rebecca before her departure.

"Read this letter, Rebecca, when I'm far away, and re-member that I love you with all my heart—you are my life. You brought light and happiness into my lonely existence," she said, handing Rebecca a small envelope.

It was hard to explain why she was afraid to read the let-ter, but one day Rebecca came across it incidentally while dusting the bookshelves. After her mother left, she tucked it away behind the books. Rebecca went to the kitchen to pre-pare supper for Igor and only then, ensconced comfortably on the sofa, pulled the letter and opened the envelope.

"*My dear beloved Rebecca, my daughter,*
How many times have I been tempted to tell you the story

of your birth, but I was too scared of losing you. You are a gift to me from God, and you gave me all the happiness in the world. It is a long story, and it is much easier for me to write than to tell it. I feel so guilty not to have told you all of this before, but believe me, Rebecca, I could not. I did not have the courage to do so. Please forgive me."

Confused, Rebecca put the letter down and wandered around the room—her thoughts in disarray. The night pressed against the window glass and crawled into the room. She picked up the letter and continued reading it, pacing the room up and down.

"I am not your mother. I found you in snow when you were just a one-month-old baby, a beautiful child I prayed for my whole adult life. My small hut stood near the Jewish cemetery. There I buried my sister and my parents who had passed away when I was only eighteen. I learned how to live alone and worked hard, trying to make both ends meet. By the time I found you, I was thirty-five years old, an old maid living alone near my deceased family. You were a miracle baby who brought happiness to my lonely dwelling.

The news that I had found a baby near the well spread fast around the town and beyond. But whose child could it be? Nobody knew or could even guess. On one cold winter day, I noticed a young man, a stranger, walking around my house. The next day he came again—he came to stay. It was your father, Samuel, who had learned that his wife abandoned you. At that time he lived in a small town called Pustoshka where he had his four brothers and many cousins. Your real mother disappeared, and nobody ever heard from her again. I do hope you'll find forgiveness in your heart. Please, understand and forgive me, my beloved daughter.
Your loving mother,
Eliza"

The drops of falling rain spattered against the window, breaking the hashed silence into the splinters of her past. Her happy childhood floated for a moment in her mind, but its vision wilted slowly away. She tried to keep these flashes from fading, to hold on to those happy days, but her memory blurred. She felt giddy from this sudden revelation. All her emotions drifted away, intertwined with the silence of the night. But then, once again, her thoughts traveled back to the day when, returning from a trip to Leningrad, she had a strange encounter.

* * * * *

The train decelerated and came to a stop. The passengers poured outside to get some food. The platform was thronged with local peasants selling pickles, sauerkraut and freshly-baked bread. Crowds were milling around the stalls with various goods. Rebecca too stepped on the platform, her arms clasped around her body to shield it from the biting northern wind blowing from an open field behind the train station.

A withered old woman, bundled up in a Russian flower-ed shawl and a heavy, ragged, quilted jacket, grabbed her by the hand. Hardship and suffering were engraved on her craggy, sallow face.

"Hi, sweetheart, don't pass me by. Just look how thin you are. Ah, ah, ah, you must be hungry. My pickles and my homemade bread are the best in the area. Give me one ruble, and they are all yours. You will not regret." She intoned and smiled at Rebecca with her toothless mouth while melo-diously stretching her words and examining Rebecca with small rheumy eyes.

"Oh, you are a beauty. Want to know your fate?" And without waiting for an answer, she opened Rebecca's palm and moved her callous fingers along the smooth surface of Rebecca's hand. "What a strange fate! You have two mo-thers. Don't you?"

Rebecca pulled her hand back. Suddenly, the woman paled and whispered something into the air, avoiding look-ing at Rebecca, "You are destined for a lamentable end, but you'll meet your fate with courage, poor girl."

Because of a freight train going by at a high speed, Rebecca could not decipher the last words, and she did not dare ask the woman to repeat, sensing something sinister in her words. However, Rebecca detected some sincere and doleful notes in the woman's voice. It was not in her manner to be disrespectful, but the woman's facial expression scared her.

"This is all nonsense. I know my past. I have only one mother. And I don't want to know my future. Besides, I don't believe in crystal-gazing. Thank you anyway. I don't need your pity. I am happy."

Rebecca was surprised at her own harshness, but she handed the old woman a ruble and took a loaf of bread, and a small jar of pickles.

She looked back and saw the train breathed out and produced a heavy puff of smoke. The conductor whistled, and she had to hurry to catch the train that had just begun to gain speed. She remained in a corridor, standing by the window for some time, watching as the boggy terrain flashed quickly before her eyes. The despondent and melancholy visage of the landscapes merged with the sky. The sun, like a fading fireball, drooped in the west, and was finally swallowed up by the earth. The last tender tints of the parting day appeared on the verge of the horizon. Twilight enveloped the earth and threw a curtain of dusk on the rutted, fast-moving landscape as the train clattered on through the night.

* * * * *

This vivid picture from her past vanished instantly when Rebecca heard steps, and then somebody inserted the key into the door lock. Her husband entered the room, carrying with him a scent of summer and a whiff of fresh air. He turned on the light, and it pushed the darkness back. Like a scared bird it flew away and into the empty street.

This sudden light brought Rebecca back from her fleeting reminiscence. Slowly, the words from the letter began to sink into Rebecca's consciousness and make some sense. She got up and without saying a word moved to the kitchen to hide the letter far back in a drawer, away from Igor. *Who was her real mother? Why did she abandon her?* All these conflicting thoughts, like annoying flies, noised in her head. She could feel cold penetrating her palms and flowing into her heart.

Was it a dream or did she hear Igor talking to her loudly, annoyed by her silence? She couldn't understand what he was saying to her as well as she couldn't comprehend the news about her birth mother.

Chapter Seven
Blue Cottage

*T*he next day, Rebecca complained to her husband on the headache, but instead of going to bed early she watched through the window how the night ebbed into nothingness, and the fathomless sky brooded low above the town, like the quiet sea resting after a storm. She didn't get a wink of sleep that night, lost in contemplation. Rebecca wandered about the house until the first rays of sun crept into the room. Her pain was slowly becoming dulled. She busied herself in the kitchen, concentrating on the sharp knocks in her belly, as if her unborn child were begging her to bring him out into this cruel world.

A short time later, Rebecca heard rumors that Igor had begun working for the Germans. She didn't want to believe it, but every time she tried to wheedle information out of him about his work, he would give her a cagey reply.

"It's none of your business after all. You have food on the table. What else do you need? Where is your gratitude?" he would snap at her.

Rebecca became aware that her neighbors were avoiding her, especially her Jewish friends and even relatives, but she didn't bother to ask why. All she could think about now was her unborn child. Oh, how much she wanted her child to have a mother, to grow up to be a strong and honest person, to make her proud, but soon the latest news made her realize—the days of her life might now be numbered.

One day, returning home from visiting her relatives, she caught sight of a big poster printed in two languages, German and Russian. It was signed by the Governor of Nevel, someone by the name of Vasiliev. She read it carefully, barely able to understand the cruelty of the written words, concerning her and all Jewish population. But when its meaning finally sank into consciousness, she was paralyzed by fear and by its tangible and shocking reality, and yet her whole being refused to believe it.

Rebecca pressed her hands to her chest and scurried home through the desolate streets. For a moment, breathing heavily, she leaned against the wall, feeling how her baby moved in her belly. Still panting for air, she stared blindly into empty space, all her energy leaving her body. She felt like a stranger in her own town, forgotten and abandoned to die. Running again for her life through the familiar streets from the brutal reality, she was finally seized by panic. Rebecca felt that those streets would never end, and their hushed quietude frightened her. Their asphalt covers shone and writhed in the ensuing dusk. She felt as if she were walking on the surface of the opaque river whose dark waters could open their abyss and swallow her forever.

A sudden crescent moon, reminding her of a lemon fruit-drop, filtered out for a moment, its smooth sheen covering the road...or the river. Rebecca stopped, scared, confused, lost. Where was she? She didn't recognize the place. Swallowing her fear, she moved forward through the dusk and begged the fruit-drop to show her the way home, away from the horror of war....

* * * * *

On August 7th, the Gestapo issued a special order for all the local Jews. German troops, armed with rifles and machine guns, cordoned off the square, named famously after

Karl Marx. It became the place where the Jewish population was forced to go for registration from all over the town and its bordering villages. There, men, women and children were wedged in one dense mass, yielding to their fate.

Meanwhile, it was announced that the punishment for hiding Jews—was death. Those Jews, who didn't obey the Nazis' orders, faced immediate execution. All these conditions spawned terror in their hearts and made them wonder if they could possibly survive the German occupation.

At the same time, in order to avoid unnecessary panic the citizens of Nevel were told that the Nazis were going to send all the Jews to Palestine. Some of the locals believed them, clutching at the last straw of hope. Many Nevel Jews appeared at the Gestapo registration post right away, not even suspecting that their fate was sealed—they were doomed and would never return to their homes. During the next two days, the first string of more than 1,000 people walked along Vitebsk Avenue towards Blue Cottage, two kilometers away from Nevel, under the watch of the Russian Chief of Police, Sepunov. Dry, irritating vortexes of dust rose around them, covering their pale, worried faces with deathly grey layers.

Before sunset, under the watch of the local policemen and dogs, the rest of the cortege arrived at Blue Cottage. The last tender tints of receding day still lingered over the horizon on the verge of impending twilight. As Blue Cottage merged with the night, its new inhabitants, including women and children, found crammed into one house. People couldn't sleep, thinking about their future. Through the windows, they saw how the armed soldiers and policemen surrounded the house, watching them as though they were criminals.

And only in the morning, could they see what a beautiful place Blue Cottage really was. It was a peaceful and remote territory with an almost serene setting. Somewhere from far away, the wind brought an odor of hay, fresh dung, and wild flowers. A big park with green alleys and tall birch trees was built in the center of the suburb near an old mansion, called

"Blue Dacha." A long, sandy alley with flowerbeds on either side led to a red brick mansion where the night before the police and Gestapo unloaded the remaining Jews. Turning Blue Cottage into the first Jewish ghetto in the Russian land, the Germans established there a rigorous regime, during which they subjected the Jews to constant torture, beatings and malicious insults.

Within the next few weeks, people lived in ignorance of what lay ahead. The children were torn away from their mothers. They couldn't pray any longer and just quietly sobbed. The sudden sticky, hot August days, cold evenings and long working hours exhausted people. Addled by Nazi lies, they now existed in a savage world, bereft of any hope of survival. They were driven to work in the city every day, but neither food nor water had been provided for them. It was hard labor, often beyond their strength. Those, who were weak and feeble, were hammered to death. Only sometimes, the local peasants, feeling deep commiseration, under the shelter of the dark nights, risking their own lives, would bring them something to eat. Hunger, frustration and the cruelty of the Nazis drained people of their strength and their belief in any sort of salvation.

Chapter Eight
Interpretation of Dreams

*B*y now, the restaurant was slowly filling up with new customers, but neither Alex nor Eduardo paid attention to the increasing noise around them. They were still absorbed in the tragedy of Nevel's population. Thick cigarette smoke now hung heavily over the tables, like smoke from the burning churches, buildings and synagogue, resurrected just some minutes ago from Alex's narrative. The shock from what he had just heard flooded Eduardo with emotion. He couldn't force himself to touch food now. He moved his plate away and put down his glass of wine. An expression of pain crossed over his face.

"Who was Rebecca? Who were Leon and Mark? Are you related? Were you born in Nevel? Tell me, Alex, is Rebecca your mother?"

"Eduardo, please don't rush me. You'll learn all of this in good time. This story is far from over. The suffering those poor people endured is indescribable. Only survivors of the horror of war are capable of understanding. My father witnessed it, and I am trying to relate it to you the way he told me the story of his family before he died."

"What an incredible fate." Eduardo shook his head. "I can't imagine life during the war with so little food and water, and death following their every step. To live in fear is the most humiliating thing that can happen to a human being. What an iniquitous world and what unspeakable crimes!"

Minutes passed before either of them could speak again.

"The power of evil should never prevail, and only we, the humans, are capable of stopping it," Eduardo continued after a short pause.

"You are such an idealist, Eduardo. Evil forces always win."

"Maybe, but what about the power of love?"

"It's only in our dreams. Has it ever happened to you that you had the same tumultuous dream all the time—distorted reality, twisted, evil images?"

Alex's question seemed to have some impact on Eduardo. "Oh, yes, but in my dreams I see no evil. I often see the same image of a young woman with the face of Madonna, lit up by an eerie inward light. She is always trying to say something to me, but every time at that very moment she disappears into obscurity, and I can only hear her voice fading away. I think I fell in love with this illusive woman from my dream a long time ago. She represented for me the chastity of our souls, the purity of the world around us. She represented Love. I have never revealed this dream to anybody before. You know, I once read that we all live different lives and have different goals and values in life, but there is one passion we all share—the passion for love. This phrase is embedded in my memory forever."

Eduardo became suddenly disconcerted at having revealed his soul to a stranger who happened to be his double.

Alex was intrigued, and at the same time very sympathetic; he recognized himself as well. He too had always searched for this ideal love.

It took some time before he replied, "Well, I read once about some techniques of dream interpretation. Maybe it will help you to decipher your dream. Sigmund Freud once wrote about the existence of a bridge from the apparently remote dream world to real life. There are memories of the past or our associations connected with something that happened a long time ago. Repressing those memories, we cause them to come to us in dreams or some kind of associations that may suddenly appear in our sleep. He wrote that while we are asleep there is an alteration and distribution of psychic energy."

Alex stopped and darted a glance at Eduardo, who listened to him carefully, leaning forward.

"Please, go on," Eduardo asked him nervously.

Alex nodded. "In a way, for me, to have a dream or to hallucinate is almost equal to painting a picture when your unconscious emotions are turned on. The same is true for love. In my opinion, it is an unconscious feeling, the fulfillment of our dreams. We are all longing for love. We are all dreamers, no matter who we are or what we expect from life. The woman from your fantasy is a personification of your dream or an image from your remote past....Could I be right?"

Eduardo threw an odd look at Alex, wondering how he had just managed to peep through his secret thoughts. "As you know, Alex, we, the artists, are all dreamers, living in our own world of illusion and images. Do you agree?"

"Yes, I agree. It is a painful process to pour your soul onto canvases. How often do people see your creation in a distorted way? You might be surprised by why I only paint the rich and famous. It does not give me any satisfaction, but it brings peace to my soul and heart. Long ago, I ceased suffering, choosing to leave behind the world of real art, the world of illusion and pain."

"You have touched a most sensitive subject that also concerns me profoundly. My process of creativity, Alex, is just the opposite. My art at the beginning was based on simplicity, superficial feelings, but ended up by baring my soul and my emotions. Fate—or perhaps just one encounter—has changed my life forever. Nevertheless, I have a feeling that we are kindred spirits with the only difference being that your soul is much stronger than mine. You escaped your pain by devoting your talent to a superficial art. You shut up your soul and use only your eyes and hands. As for me, I pour all my grief, all my dissatisfaction, all my disillusionment onto canvas in hopes of easing my suffering. In everyday life, I wear a mask to deceive the world, and probably I do manage to conceal the true nature of my unhappiness. I often think that our unhappiness has its roots in our childhood or unfulfilled feelings. Don't you think so, Alex?"

Alex gazed at Eduardo, realizing his double at last was going to talk about his past.

"Well, I never saw my father. He died on the day I was born. My mother loved me unconditionally and struggled to give me a good education. I had an incredible passion for painting. As I mentioned to you before, I was born in Austria, but I grew up in Italy, first in Florence, then in Rome, surrounded by the art of the greatest Italian masters."

It seemed now that Eduardo plunged into his own thoughts and was speaking only to himself, as if taking no notice of Alex's presence. Alex thought about the notebook. It made sense now. The man was probably tormented by his past, by his unhappy childhood. But exactly what was his childhood and what was his life? Who was this mysterious man, his mirror image?

"Eduardo, you haven't yet told me much about yourself. Who was your father? Is your mother still alive? Do you have a family?" He felt that Eduardo wanted to tell him something but could not yet bring himself to trust Alex.

Eduardo repressed a beguiling smile. "Humph, you popped quite a bold question, my friend, considering our short acquaintance. My mother died two years ago, hoping before her death to see my great success. I was married once but divorced after only three years of marriage. I have a son, his name is Marco, and he is a grown man. I have never remarried, although I was once deeply in love," he replied rather scornfully. "Somehow, I don't like to talk about my life or to dramatize the events that took place many years ago."

Never before had it occurred to Eduardo to tell his story to anybody. He gave up thinking about his past a long time ago. Once, it seemed to be so significant—the past that had changed his life and his views on art, but with time it had become almost like a spectral past, a shadow…until today….

He leaned back in his chair, and a vague smile touched the corners of his lips. Once again, the image of the woman he once loved glowed vividly in his mind. He hesitated for a moment before he began talking.

"As a matter of fact, this very hotel evoked some reminiscence, a brief happenstance that took place a long time ago and made an indelible impression on my work, and my life," Eduardo confided.

He paused and, peering into the distance above Alex's head, as if looking back into his past, began his story: "To be exact, it happened about twenty years ago here in New York. I hope it won't be too tedious for you to listen to my boring story."

"No, not at all," Alex vigorously protested, "please, continue. I am eager to know as much as possible about you. After all, we could be somehow connected."

Eduardo nodded obligingly and managed a faint smile.

"Splendid. I am glad that you display such a keen interest in my life. Well, going back to my love story….You will be surprised to learn that in addition to being an artist I graduated from the Academia National di Santa Cecilia in Rome and at that time was known in the musical world."

He moved his plate farther away and took a gulp of wine as if trying to clear his throat. "I didn't mention this to you, but I have been composing music as long as I have been painting. Those were two of my passions. So, here it goes…. That day in December…."

Chapter Nine
Blizzard in New York

*T*hat day in December Eduardo had a ticket for a concert at Carnegie Hall. The program included Brahms, Rachmaninoff and Tchaikovsky, his favorite composers. He planned to stay in New York only for a couple of days on his way to Washington, where he was going to visit some of his fellow artists, and then fly back to Rome. However, he learned in the morning that it was going to be a cold and windy day. A severe snowstorm was forecasted by nightfall. Therefore, the much-anticipated concert was suddenly cancelled. Now he regretted having come to New York in such stormy weather. Although his day was ruined, Eduardo still tried to justify his unnecessary stop in this city. The prospect of spending a day by himself made him feel miserable. He loathed staying in the hotel alone imprisoned in a small cell. Therefore, he decided to spend a day at the Metropolitan Museum of Art.

He was surprised to see that despite the blizzard and bitterly cold weather, the Metropolitan Museum was crowded with people milling about and pushing each other, and the stoically standing museum guards. Museums and art galleries were always his sacred places where in total solitude he could observe the mystery of art, and feel the deep spirituality depicted in paintings by artists of past centuries. Most of all, he loved paintings by Tintoretto and Botticelli for the warmth of their gold colors, purity of their tones, clarity and smoothness of their brush strokes. A woman in Botticelli's paintings became the woman of his dream, attracting him by her warm, tender femininity. Sometimes, he saw her in his imagination—transparently gold, flying with him into quiet, deep and unfathomable skies. He often tried to find her in the real world but could only find her shadow or distorted image.

Even now, listlessly watching the crowd, in one sweeping glance he noticed a young woman in the ticket line. She seemed to be preoccupied with her thoughts, and he detected an expression of sadness on her face. While everything was moving around her, she looked quite alone, isolated within the large crowd, remaining in her own world.

Nothing is more disturbing than to feel lonely in a large crowd, he thought while examining her expression. Usually, Eduardo was not so easily impressed. After his bitter divorce, he finally realized that he didn't need any special woman to change his happy and placid life. He immersed himself in his own world of art and music, and only an occasional love affair distracted him from the one thing he loved most—his work. But the aura of mystery that emanated from this stranger, aroused his curiosity. A sudden, scarcely acknowledged desire, took some unpredictably possession of him. Without thinking twice, haunted by her image, he decided to follow her.

The woman bought a ticket and then, pausing just for a moment, hurried toward the new exhibition of the Spanish artist Jusepe de Ribera. It was exactly what he had planned. Eduardo was delighted—they had the same intention, and he hastened gaily after her. He stumbled upon the woman at the very first painting. She was leaning forward, carefully studying the portrait of an old man. Eduardo, moved by simple curiosity, began to scrutinize her—his eyes traveling from her face down her body. She was of average height, slim, well-built. He was struck by something childlike in her whole appearance. He continued to examine her. She had long chestnut hair, falling down to her shoulders in soft waves, setting off her delicate and yet dusky complexion. She was dressed in a black turtleneck sweater and blue jeans, holding a short fur jacket in her hands. She looked very appealing in her simple outfit.

"Like it? I do. What say you?" Eduardo asked, bending affably closer to her face.

He inhaled a faint scent of some refined perfume. The woman raised her eyes then gazed at him with a prolonged, remote and absentminded look, nodded and turned away, unconcerned. She totally ignored him and his question. Eduardo was unpleasantly surprised by her rudeness. He didn't go away but instead observed her eyes of a soft, hazel color with golden lights, inviting him to drown in their mysterious depth. Intrigued, he still patiently waited for her reply, wondering if it was impolite of him to start a conversation with a stranger, but after all he was an Italian, and she was an attractive woman. Almost a whole minute passed before she looked at him again and smiled. And suddenly, her whole face lit up with the same familiar inner light he had seen before on the faces of women painted by Sandro Botticelli.

"Oh….I do know you and love you very much," she prattled and then added in embarrassment, "I mean I love your work and the way you express yourself in your paintings, and in your music. You are Eduardo Goldano, the Italian artist and composer, aren't you? Or…maybe you have just reminded me of someone? Actually, you really do…."

"In fact, you are right—I am Eduardo Goldano, your humble servant, but how do you know my name?" Now it was his turn to be surprised.

"I saw one of your exhibitions in Rome and fell in love with your work. Your originality and the anguish of your turbulent colors shone through your work and were magnetizing. The emotions, the disturbing colors, strong brush and sensitive soul impressed me the most. When I looked at your work, I knew exactly what you felt when you painted your pictures. I even had a chance to exchange some words with you," she exhaled and blushed like a schoolgirl.

"Oh, right now I feel that once and for all I have achieved immortality. Did I really make such an indelible impression on you? I am honored."

She blushed again, avoiding his eyes. Eduardo gave a heartfelt chuckle, bowed, and a roguish twinkle danced in his eyes.

"May I ask your name?"

"I am Nora," she announced somewhat tersely and stretched her hand for shaking. Her hand was small and soft. This innocent gesture roused his curiosity about her all the more.

They walked for hours through the exhibition together, exchanging their thoughts and opinions. It appeared that they had the same taste in art. One of Ribera's portraits impressed them both, and drew them into conversation.

"For Ribera," Nora reasoned, "in my opinion, spiritual beauty and intellect were more important than physical appearance. Look at his portraits. They are of incomparable artistry. On the one hand, one could be struck by the physical ugliness of his sitters; on the other hand—impressed by their deep spirituality. Take for example the portrait of this philosopher. It is my favorite. Do you agree?"

They approached the portrait she had pointed out to him. It was as if she read his mind. His perception of the painting was identical. Their feelings about art bound them together. They began to feel at ease with one another. It happens sometimes in life that you meet someone and suddenly sense with all your heart, subconsciously, that it was fated.

Chapter Ten
Farewell

*E*duardo and Nora left the museum together. By then the snowstorm had ended, but a high wind dashed into their faces. The ground was crusted over with deep layers of snow, and the roofs of the buildings were mantled and capped with ice. The brittle branches, crackling in the wind were frosted with icicles. The last fading sunrays reflected in their transparent purity and looked like imaginary precious stones or even like large, sparkling diamonds. Eduardo took one tiny icicle in his hand, and it slowly melted, turning into droplets of water.

"I wanted to give you a diamond ring, but it disappeared just before my generous gesture could be realized. I almost proposed to you."

"Don't worry, just look how many huge diamonds are hanging from the roofs."

She had scarcely finished her sentence when a long, heavy icicle fell to the ground next to them. Barely escaping, they laughed. The northern wind increased its speed, and the temperature fell sharply. However, they did not feel the cold—their hearts were on fire.

As they wandered about the quiet streets of New York, she spoke to him in a soft voice, showing her interest in his art and music. She felt free to express her opinion about his musical compositions.

"Remember what Shelley once wrote: 'They learn in suffering what they teach in song.' I think that, compared with your paintings, your music lacks profundity."

Eduardo was shocked and even annoyed with her bold, straightforward statements, though he appreciated her honesty.

"Let me make it clear. Are you trying to suggest that the creative process is based on suffering, and that those, who have not suffered, are incapable of creating? Do you really mean what you're saying?" He reacted quickly.

She sensed some irritation in his voice and replied hastily. "Yes, I do think that the real, profound art comes from profound suffering. I am talking about suffering that leaves deep scars on our souls. Thomas Eliot once wrote that to write poetry does not mean to express but to escape yourself. When creative people put their thoughts and emotions on paper, they cleanse their hearts and souls, they share their experience with the rest of the world. What is it, our experience? Our experience is what we learn through suffering."

"It's interesting what you are saying. I have never thought about it before, but you are probably right. I eventually give up," he admitted rather gleefully, "but your observation made me analyze why sadness has always been a part of my soul."

Nora nodded in sympathy.

"First, I am an artist and then a composer. I feel and comprehend art at much deeper level than music, and it is much closer to my heart and my soul. I will not argue with you about 'depth of creativity.' I need to think about it. You might be right."

And in his usual manner, he leaned forward and almost whispered, "I don't mean to pry, don't take me wrong, but it is your turn now to tell me about yourself. One subject that we have not touched on yet is you. Do you mind telling me your story?"

He fixed his green eyes on her. She seemed somewhat reluctant to talk, but finally drawing a deep breath, she asked him uncertainly, "What would you like to know? Honestly, there is not much to say."

"Anything and everything...."

Nora slowed her steps and, after some hesitation, began talking, looking straight in front of her.

"I live in Philadelphia, and I came to New York for just two days to see the exhibition and simply to spend a day in my favorite museum. I needed some time to be alone in order to make a decision that may change my life forever. What else?"

She seemed lost in reverie for some time. He didn't interrupt her, waiting patiently for her to continue the story. He felt some latent, heartfelt warmth emanating from her. He began to feel deep down that he did, indeed, need a woman like Nora in his life—a person with cordiality, warmth and understanding.

"Look, Eduardo, I don't really know what else to tell you."

She walked silently next to him. The wind strolled pensively behind them, wiping carefully their footsteps and eavesdropping curiously on their conversation.

"Do you have a man in your life?" He inquired, while recognizing that he was probably a damned fool for asking such a question of someone who was little more than a stranger. But he felt that the woman walking next to him was not a stranger anymore. He realized that there was a deep connection, a strong, invisible bond between the two of them.

"Yes, I do," she blurted out unexpectedly, "That's all I can tell you. Our relations are too complicated, and truly, I am not in the mood to discuss it, especially today and now." Nora seemed visibly upset, as if he touched the subject she was not inclined to discuss.

Coming closer to her, Eduardo pressed her elbow as if trying to let her know that he understood. He wanted to show her how much he needed her and her closeness at this moment. The unspoken words, deep, mutual understanding, inner longing for each other united them in that cold, winter blizzard.

"There is something awfully moving about you, Nora. It may sound odd, but when you look at me, I have the feeling that you are looking deep into my mind. Do you also have feel that we are inwardly bonded? It seems to me so unusual that we grew up in different countries and yet have so much in common."

She didn't reply, and he didn't wait for her answer. She freed herself and slowed her pace, quiet and rueful, while he was watching her being engrossed in her own thoughts.

How could she know that for him this lonely, cold night and a beautiful woman with chestnut, golden hair were like a miracle recreated by the brush of the mysterious Italian painter Sandro Botticelli?

* * * * *

The city had already drifted into slumber, and even the windows had shut their wide-open eyes. Eventually, pitch darkness embraced the city and its tall buildings. Large, heavy icicles still dangled from windowsills, threatening to break off and fall. Everyone seemed to be hiding in their warm, cozy dwellings, and it was only the two of them who were aimlessly rambling through the empty streets of New York, reluctant and unwilling to say goodbye to each other. Finally, they found a small restaurant, half-empty at the hour. In the corner, an old man quietly played a piano, a tango from the movie *Gilda* that Nora loved. She smiled and took his hand. Eduardo could not take his eyes off Nora's face. He felt an immense physical attraction for her. Struggling to conceal his emotions, he forced himself to take the first step.

"We don't have much time left, Nora", he was searching for the right words, "maybe just this one night." He gave her a swift glance as she again trustfully touched his hand across the table.

"Look, Nora," he spoke rapidly, afraid that she would interrupt his train of thoughts, "why don't you move your luggage to my hotel room? We can spend more time together. Never in my life had I felt so attracted to a woman I hardly knew."

"The truth is, Eduardo, that before long you'll forget me. I am nobody or maybe just that tiny star that soon will merge with the universe."

He didn't reply because he didn't know what to say to her. He felt pity in his heart for himself, for this seemingly casual and yet such an unusual adventure. He wanted to think that it was indeed just a moment of passion, afraid to give their feelings a proper name—love.

At this very moment, they were both engulfed by sudden intensity of emotions, the uncertainty of their future, difficulties to come to the right conclusion. He had to make only one step forward and she would give up everything, but he saw the impossibility to make such a step, afraid to ruin her happy life, her and his own future. He still could not apprehend the depth of their spiritual and physical connection, the meaning of their sudden feelings.

"Eduardo, when you return to Italy, I want you always remember me as the illusive woman from the New York blizzard."

"I wish for you to be real. What had happened to us is real. Maybe one day the fate will bring us together again. I want to hope."

"I don't know, Eduardo. Time will tell."

"But then it could be too late."

"Don't torture yourself. I wish it were in our power to change the circumstances, to have enough courage to give up everything for the one you love. Are you capable of doing so? Look deep inside your soul. But is it love? Maybe what happened to us is just a flash of light."

She desperately wanted to hear a different answer when he replied rather stiffly.

"You are right. Life is too complicated, selfish. Perhaps it could be just a fleeting feeling. Maybe we should be happy with what we have today. Nobody can predict tomorrow. Let's wait, time will decide for us."

"I have no time, Eduardo. Tomorrow my life will change forever. I don't know how to express my gratitude to you for this marvelous day we have spent together. Thank you."

Impulsively, she rose and stepped toward him. He took her into his arms. Their lips locked in prolong, passionate kiss. He finally let her go and cleared his throat. Then they both fell into silence, but some important, still unspoken words hung in the air. When he began talking, he heard his own voice as if it were spoken by another person.

"I don't want you to go. I can't say goodbye. The realization I will never see you again is becoming too painful."

He could not find a reason to convince her to stay. He kept talking as if trying to fill a space between them, to prolong the time, their last moments together.

They left the restaurant and turned around the corner. Nora suddenly stopped.

"Maybe it should be this way. It is too late anyway. I wish I had never met you. We are on the road of no-return," she said quietly.

"Well, I suppose so," he nodded, following her. He was deeply hurt, but pride didn't allow him to beg her to leave her previous life and go with him to Italy. Eduardo always lived by impulse, trusting his intuition. However, this time it was only his pride that kept him silent.

"I am leaving soon for Italy and you return to Philadelphia, I can't insist. After all, your whole life is there. You hardly know me. I live by emotions, but I trust my instinct. I feel with all my heart—you are my woman, and you are the one to make a decision whether to stay with me or to go back to your previous life."

Nora did not reply. She walked away from him. Eduardo came close but didn't dare to ask for her address or phone number—a decision he would lately regret.

"I'll see you off, Nora."

"No, please. I would rather say goodbye to you now. I'll catch a cab right here. Take care of yourself, Eduardo. I will not forget you."

"Never in my life had I felt that way. I will always remember you, Nora. I hope you will be happy with the man you are going to marry. I wish you...." He almost choked and stopped talking, looking away from her.

"I had a feeling, Nora, that I had known you long before we met, and that we were just reunited after so many years of separation." He swallowed his pride once again.

Nora did not say a word but took off a glove and extended her hand to say goodbye. Only then did his eyes catch the glimmer of a large diamond engagement ring on her right hand. She saw his gaze and hastily pulled her hand back. She was about to leave when suddenly she turned around, and an odd expression flickered across her face.

"Your eyes are of such an unusual color, neither grey nor blue. I would say slate-colored," she paused, "or even sometimes they are the color of aquamarine stone. That's right—stone. I have seen such a color before, but it was usually icy cold. We should not see each other again, Eduardo, ever."

She shot him a frosty look and then waved for an approaching taxi. He didn't have time to reply. She hopped into a cab that was about to take her away from him forever...

Chapter Eleven
"To Nora"

"*A*t night, we sink into fairytale dreams of an unreal world, and it's only when waking up in the morning that we realize the reality of today and our solitude in this immense space and time," Eduardo said pensively on finishing his story and then cited Heinrich Heine:

> *Outside, white snowflakes* are blowing
> *Through the night: the storm is loud:*
> *Here I'm alone, besides the blazing*
> *Hearth inside, warm, quietly bowed.*
> *I sit here in my chair, just thinking,*
> *Here beside the crackling glow,*
> *Kettle humming, as it's boiling,*
> *Melodies from long ago.*

Alex recognized his favorite German poet and continued citing the verses.

> *Now many a long forgotten age*
> *Rises in the twilight air,*
> *As if in shining masquerade,*
> *And faded splendor, there.*

"How shocking it is that we both can recite the same poem." Eduardo smiled rather absentmindedly, having some difficulty within his mind as he crossed the border from his distant past and to the present.

"Did you ever see her again?" Alex inquired.

"No, I did not. Remember that I did not even ask her whereabouts." Eduardo shook his head.

"Have you ever tried to find her?"

Eduardo said nothing. He was seemingly disturbed by these questions, and it became obvious to Alex that he was not inclined to continue discussing this painful subject. Since the time of her leave taking, whenever during his long lonely evenings he thought about Nora, Eduardo remained deeply troubled by those old memories. After all, at this very moment Eduardo could hardly grasp the idea that he had just revealed his innermost feelings to a stranger. Or was Alex a stranger?

"Please, Alex, continue your story. What happened next? I have a strange feeling that...."

"Don't you feel tired? Alex turned to Eduardo.

"Why? I am perfectly fine."

"Look, Eduardo, we are both tired out. It's getting late. Why not save the rest of our story for tomorrow? I'll continue it at breakfast and tell you all I know about the fate of my family. We can ask at the desk if there are still any rooms available at this hotel, so you can stay the night. Let's get out of here."

Eduardo finished his wine in a gulp and nodded agreeably, but he was visibly disappointed by this abrupt ending.

The lobby of the hotel was empty except for an old couple who were arguing loudly with the receptionist. The old man with a sharp nose and small eyes peered at the recaptionist, scrutinizing her with disdain while his wife stood aside, evidently ashamed of her husband's loud behavior.

"Never again in my lifetime will I come back to your hotel! What kind of room did you give us?! All the windows face a noisy street. Please move us to a better room, or perhaps call another hotel and check if they have a room for us," the old man screamed, looking extremely upset. He angrily threw the key from his room on the counter.

Alex winked at Eduardo. "I see that our luck is now resting on this counter. Do you mind a noisy room?"

"Are you kidding me, Alex? I am dead tired. I could even sleep in this lobby. I wouldn't mind moving into that awful room right away."

By the time the receptionist had settled her dispute with the old couple, Eduardo had his lucky key for the noisy room which happened to be right above Alex's suite. Finally, they decided to meet the following morning at nine o'clock downstairs at the same restaurant so Alex could continue delivering the story that had taken place almost sixty years ago. They were both excited by this sudden turn of events, and each felt the closeness that sometimes only strangers can experience after long and heartfelt effusions.

* * * * *

Since their long conversation ended late, Eduardo felt exhausted. He took a long, hot shower and stretched out comfortably in bed, hoping to get some sleep, but instead he lay awake, mulling over his own hapless life.

On one rainy day, yielding to his mood, he sat at the piano and played her favorite prelude by Chopin. The sound of the raindrops and the outside noise—everything dissolved in his music. It seemed the entire orchestra, revealing a new palette of sounds, played it. He felt as if he were playing a new symphony, the raging symphony of his life. The sounds scattered and then united again, plunging into the air and eventually dying. He closed the cover of the piano, moved the chair closer to the fireplace and added some wood. The room grew much warmer. The music still disturbed him, but the new composition had already been born in his head. He knew he should get up and write down the scores, but he was incapacitated, unable to move, to break the warmth of the hot air, to lose the sounds of music and scare this fragile sense of the past. It was pleasant and yet disturbing.

At last, he sat at the piano again. The room, the furniture, everything disappeared, and only the red sparkles from the fireplace remained. The music poured out without any difficulties—hot and spiritual, light and complicated, like his life, like his feelings for her. The music filled the air with the commotion, the dramatic cords and the sudden changes into the soft, languid tones. The wind grew silent, and the curtains no longer moved. The fireplace stopped cracking. Everything fell into silence, as if listening to this sudden profound and tragic symphony. He finished playing and looked throughout the scores. He was longing to repeat the music, but all his strength had left him. In front of the title he put his dedication "To Nora." This was the only music Eduardo had ever dedicated to her....

Eduard had been happy once, though it was all in the past. He did not watch time anymore. All the events, people, everything, moved around him while he remained frozen in that time when he was so deeply in love with a woman who belonged to another man....

* * * * *

When Alex walked into the restaurant the following morning, Eduardo was already at the table, clean-shaven and neatly dressed. He was drinking his coffee, nervously looking at his watch.

"Good morning, Eduardo," Alex greeted him warmly, shaking his hand.

Eduardo rose with a wide but sad smile on his face. "I'm so glad to see you, Alex."

"Sorry to be late. I had a bad dream. Did you sleep well?"

Alex glanced imploringly at Eduardo and was flabbergasted to see that his face looked tired after an evidently sleepless night.

"Thank you for asking, Alex. No, not really. I hardly slept at all, subsiding once in a while into a fitful slumber. But every time I woke up, I was thinking about the story that you began to tell me. Please go on. I am eager to know what happened next."

Alex relaxed for a minute, concentrating. Finally, he gathered his thoughts and returned to the narrative he had to interrupt the previous evening.

"So, I told you about Blue Cottage, the first Jewish Ghetto in the Russian land. On the same day the Jewish people were driven to Blue Cottage, Igor stomped into the house and sat heavily down on the sofa, ignoring his wife's presence...."

Chapter Twelve
Unforgiveness

*O*n the same day when the Jewish people were driven to Blue Cottage, Igor stomped into the house and sat heavily down on the sofa, ignoring his wife's presence

Seeing the tormented expression on his face, Rebecca knew he brought tragic news. She had been expecting it to happen for days now, but still she felt scared.

"Tell me, Igor, what's wrong," she begged him, sitting next to him on the sofa.

"To my great chagrin, Rebecca, I have to bring you bad news. Very bad news....There is a new order today to deliver all the remaining Jews to Blue Cottage." He paused. "But I can reassure you that you can stay due to my connections to the Gestapo."

However, he tried to shield from her the whole truth.

"Yes, I heard about it. Is there an inkling of truth in your constant lies, Igor?" She moved away from him. "Do you really have any connections to the Gestapo? If you do, shame on you. I don't need your help then. Shall I start packing?"

"You want to know the truth. Fine! I am informing you that all the remaining citizens of Nevel have to register immediately at the German Command Post. But, Rebecca, for the sake of our future baby, I want to protect you, to save both of you. Your defiance surprises me, please don't be so stubborn. You are not in danger. Trust me, you are not." He gave her a warning smile.

"I don't trust you anymore, Igor. I need time to think about what to do next."

"You can think, Rebecca, but don't act against common sense. Nothing terrible is going to happen to us. I promise. Think about our baby."

She threw a wistful gaze at her husband and walked outside, feeling woozy from an agonizing pain that racked her whole body. A German rocket soared up into the sky and loudly exploded somewhere in the lake, just behind the neighboring houses. Rebecca watched the ominous glow in anguish. Since the war had taken a complete possession of their lives, she now often tried to banish from her mind any thoughts of their uncertain future.

* * * * *

Learning from Igor the latest news, Rebecca couldn't stand by idly. Reckless of consequences, under the cover of the night, risking her life, she set off to secretly visit her aunt. Since the German troops occupied Nevel, there was no sign of life on its streets. She ran, hiding behind the dark houses, dissolving in the shadows of high trees, keeping distance from the populated areas. Finally, she managed to reach her aunt's backyard safely. She stood for some time at the front door of the old familiar house mantled with heavy fog and surrounded by wooded area. It was a dark summer night. The earth evaporated evening chill. She began feeling giddiness from a heady smell emanated from the woods, although the air was cold as it usually happened when you got into the wooded area. She knocked at the door and called her aunt's name. The woman popped out of the window and stared into the night. Rebecca stood at the doorsteps, blinking, while the fear of being caught still smoldered in her heart.

"It's me, auntie. I hope I didn't wake you up." Rebecca whispered but loud enough that her aunt could hear her.

The woman came out. She could not conceal her astonishment at seeing Rebecca. Her ash-gray face expressed deep distress. First, she carefully examined the yard, pierced her eyes into the dark wooded area and only then let Rebecca in.

"No, you didn't wake us up. We are packing, but you shouldn't come, Rebecca. It's too dangerous."

She embraced the girl and quickly ushered her into the room. She was thunderstruck by Rebecca's bravery. Rebecca stood in the middle, surveying the room in bewilderment. Her aunt's usually neat house was a mess—all their belongings were littered about in total disarray. Children, looking lost and scared, sat quietly around the table. Her heart withered as she watched the scene—her relatives packing for a long trip to Palestine, refusing to accept the inevitable—their demise. Rebecca hugged warmly every one of them.

"Don't go," she begged them, "Please don't go. Hide into the woods. Hide somewhere. I'll help you as much as I can."

But they didn't hear her—they put their trust in God and God only.

"He will not let us die. He'll take care of us, of you, of your baby," her aunt said, evading Rebecca's intense, worried look.

Now bereft of any hope, Rebecca turned to her aunt's oldest daughter, Roza, who was also her closest friend. She was three years younger than Rebecca, considered being a real beauty with smooth skin and large murky eyes. She was the most popular girl in their school, but today her face was a greenish pallor. Rebecca took her aside. Roza seemed to be deeply upset by a sudden turn of events.

Rebecca made an attempt to appeal to her conscience, "Roza, I beg of you not to go. I feel with all my heart the danger awaiting all of us."

"Don't worry, Rebecca, we are all going to be send to Palestine. I am sure. Nothing, nothing is going to happen to us," she tried to convince Rebecca, but her words sounded very unconvincing.

At daybreak Rebecca kissed every one of them, knowing in her heart that she would never see them again.

Autumn had just begun to paint the woods with beautiful varieties of colors. Swaths of new-shorn grass gave her a feeling of a peaceful country life, but the piles of broken glass, furniture, debris of all kind of lumber painted quite a different picture. She hesitated for a moment but then decided it would be safer to return home by taking a short cut through the cemetery.

Rebecca walked fast, looking back with the strange feeling, as if someone was following her, breathing heavily onto her neck. But it was just the light breeze, playing its games with her, pattering, groaning, and laughing. Heavy gravel rustled under her feet. Somewhere far-off, but distinct, an owl whooped out a strident, drawling cry. Rebecca flinched and peeked around cautiously to see if someone had been following her, but she didn't see anybody. The pale moonlight swam on the surface of the sky, struggling to break the white mass of heavy clouds. The soft lilac light shimmered down upon the cemetery, creating an eerie sensation of total solitude. She was approaching her house when in the fading away moonlight she noticed a dark shadow flickered round the corner.

"Who is there?" Whispered Rebecca, trying to pierce through the fog. An unknown woman appeared in front of her, calling her by name, "Rebecca, Rebecca."

Rebecca stopped, glancing at a stranger. The woman was probably in her late forties. Her well-shaped oval face with a perfect marble skin was framed by the heavy, ash-blond hair tied behind with a pin. Her wide-opened blue eyes set deep in their sockets, and only her thin lips made a feeble attempt to stretch into a friendly smile. She was dressed in a long black skirt, and a long shawl drooped down from her shoulders. In her dark clothes, she almost merged with the dusk, like a nocturnal sorceress from Rebecca's favorite fairytale. There was something tragic and yet familiar in her face, as if she had seen her before, long ago, in her childhood imagination.

"Please, Rebecca, don't go away but listen to me," the dark woman begged.

"Have you been following me?"

"Yes and no, I have been waiting for you near the cemetery for many hours. I am sorry if I scared you. I didn't mean to do it at all."

Finally, the moonlight traveled away, and the first sunlight forced its way through the clouds. Rebecca stood for a minute contemplating.

"Please come in. My husband is not at home, and we can talk there." Rebecca took the key from the pocket of her dress and opened the door, inviting the woman in. The silence of the house oppressed the stranger for a minute. The woman stood at the doorway, shifting from one foot to the other, not knowing what to do next.

"Would you like a cup of tea?" Rebecca's voice cut off the harsh muteness as she opened the window to let fresh air in.

"Oh, no, please, don't" the woman protested, "please, please, Rebecca, close the window. Somebody could be listening to us." In a fright, she covered her face with her shawl.

"There is nobody there. Only the wind is swaying the tree branches," Rebecca tried to calm the woman. "What about tea?" She repeated her question, still carefully examining the stranger.

"No, thank you, but please listen to me. I walked from afar to see you, Rebecca, because I needed to talk to you." She took the shawl off her shoulders and threw it on the back of her chair, covering the first fine threads of sun with the transparent veil of the dark fabric.

Rebecca was thoroughly baffled. "Who are you, and how do you know my name? What can I really do for you?"

The woman continued talking as if she hadn't heard Rebecca's question, "Thus far, I have never told anybody my story. I kept my secret deep in my heart. Throughout my whole life I have been devoured by guilt." She panted for breath and then continued, "I was married when I was eighteen. My husband was the handsomest and the smartest man in the village. We lived then in a place called Pustoshka. He was the only son of the local rabbi, well-mannered and well-educated. I was lucky to have him. When my child was born, I felt as if I was the happiest woman in the world, until one day...." The woman's voice became faltering as she struggled to breath. A lurid paleness set upon her skin.

"I can't talk anymore. It is hard for me to rake over the old ashes. No, I didn't kill anybody, Rebecca, don't look at me with your fearful eyes. I lost my family, but I didn't kill anybody. Nevertheless, I made a grave mistake." She wheezed and stopped talking.

"Please continue. I want to help you if I can." Rebecca put her arms around the woman's shoulders.

"I must finish my story, Rebecca. I want you to understand me and to forgive."

Suddenly, sensing the truth, Rebecca moved away from the woman. Something struck her—she too, the only one in their family, had a perfect marble skin, ash-blond hair and blue eyes.

The woman grasped for the air. "So, one day a fortune-teller stopped me at the local market. 'You have a beautiful child,' she exclaimed, staring at my baby and grabbing me by the hand, 'but this child will sunder you from your husband. Be careful with this baby. Get rid of her.' Strangely enough, her prediction did not surprise me one whit. The big penetrating eyes of my daughter scared the hell out of me. I couldn't sleep that night. I was very superstitious, and I had to make a choice between my husband and my baby. I have chosen my husband....God punished me for that...and I have lost him too." The woman stopped talking, and for the first time looked Rebecca straight into the eyes.

"Can you forgive me, Rebecca? I am lonely and unhappy. Please forgive me, my child. I have suffered enough, and I hope God has already forgiven me, pardoned me my crime."

Rebecca came closer and bent over the woman, touching gently her hair. "For all these days, I have been struggling to understand you, but I could not. I feel sorry for you; my soul is crying, but yet deep in my heart I can't find the forgiveness."

The woman looked at Rebecca, trying to say something, hardly moving her lips. Rebecca bent over again and heard her words: "I understand. I don't blame you, Rebecca. We are two strangers on a train heading to nowhere, or...perhaps...to our demise. You heard what is going on around us. We are all going to die, all of us, but before I did hope you would be able to find in your heart compassion and forgiveness."

"I tried," Rebecca's voice wavered, and she pronounced her words with the utmost severity, "I tried to find forgiveness in my heart...but I couldn't. You left me in the snow to die. You gave me life and then tried to take it away from me. Why? What have I done to you? I haven't conceived of your actions. Would you, yourself, be able to forgive such a crime? Would you?"

The woman didn't reply. She whispered something under her breath with the muffled, hoarse voice. Rebecca couldn't understand a word of it. The woman spoke only to herself, plunged into her own world, forgetting about Rebecca and everything that kept her alive. The world around her became now strange and remote, not the same world where she had cherished her last tiny hope. She peeked listlessly at Rebecca.

"For all that, think about me, Rebecca. Never forget that

somewhere in the universe there is a lonely soul that loves you."

The woman stretched her hand and with a blind movement tenderly touched Rebecca's face. At this moment, her eyes warmed, and a guilty smile played at the corners of her lips. She sat mutely for a time, her head down. Then she surveyed the room as if trying to prolong her stay. Though not able to find the right word to express her sorrow, she got up and wrapped her shawl around her shoulders. Once more she turned into a black sorceress from the old fairytale. Making a sloping stagger toward the door, the woman looked at Rebecca for the very last time and receded into the mist of the awakening morning.

Chapter Thirteen
Playing with Death

*T*he following morning, Igor received a new assignment from the SS to take the rest of the local Jews to Blue Cottage, an order that made him fear for the life of his wife.

On the last day of the assignment, a long line of the remaining Jews went a different route. Instead of taking the main street, leading directly to Blue Cottage, the cortege lumbered out onto a country road that followed the bend of the river. Accompanied by horse-driven carts, loaded with children, old men and women, they walked along the river toward their destiny. White, tall birches, wounded by the war, flanked the road on both sides. Soon, the road turned sharply left and the horses cantered down the slope along the meandering river. They were approaching a bridge, straddling the riverbed

As if foreseeing their destiny, an old Jewish man with a grey beard and a quick eye, clutching to his heart the Holy Scriptures, gazed down on the mirrored surface of the river. The reflection of his kind old face drowned in the pitch-dark gloom of the water.

"Damn this war!" he whispered angrily, and then his pensive face turned into a sorrowful expression. He exhaled the words of prayer in Hebrew, pronouncing the blessing for survival, illness and danger:

"Barukh ata Adonai Eloheinu melekh ha-olam, ha-gomel lahayavim tovot sheg'malani kol tov."[2]

And the heart-rending prayer sounded like his last words of farewell and his last words of gratitude to the Lord whom he worshipped and loved. But in the middle of the bridge, the flow of the old man's heartfelt words had been abruptly in-terrupted.

At the beginning of the prayer, a young Russian police-man was motionless, gripping his weapon between his knees. Slowly, the words began to reach his consciousness. Infuriated by the prayer, he pushed the old man in front and pointed the gun at him.

"Старый дурак, никакой Бог тебе уже не может помочь. Я тебя сейчас проучу!"[3] He shouted at the top of his lungs, and with those words whipped out a pistol, cocked it and fired at the old man, the bullet hitting the old man in the head.

Suddenly, as if by a special order, the policemen began firing at those who were sick or old, ruthlessly pushing their bodies, dead or alive, into the river Emenka. They fell straight into the water, and the dark river turned red. Opening its abyss, it swallowed the innocent victims. Everything happened so fast that not a sound was heard, just some sudden splashes and tremulous ripples on the quietly flowing waters. A red glow billowed out above it, and the surface of the river bubbled and groaned for a long time. The river Emenka had become Nevel's first mass Jewish grave.

Time froze for a moment, as if caught in a battle between life and death. At that very instant, Igor's whole life turned upside-down. He didn't participate, but this kind of madness deeply scared him. After all, he was not a murderer, and

---

[2] "Blessed are You, LORD, our God, King of the Universe, Who bestows good things on the unworthy, and has bestowed on me every goodness." (translated from Hebrew)

[3] The old fool, the Lord can't help you anymore. And I'll teach you a lesson. (translated from Russian)

he was not going to curry favor with the Nazis. He was neither going to become a quisling nor had he any intention of betraying those to whom he owned his life and his gratitude. He made a sudden realization that his trust in German virtue was an irreparable and calamitous mistake. He was still too young and too naïve to understand that he had too became a victim of the cruel Nazis propaganda.

* * * * *

At the end of August, Rebecca gave premature birth to their son Alek. The baby was very weak and tiny but alive. Igor couldn't be happier, and yet he was afraid that someone might denounce Rebecca. He tried to hide the birth of his son from the Nazis and the local policemen. Often, his new assignment kept him away from home for days and nights.

Rebecca was overwhelmed with joy and grief at the same time, sensing the approaching end. At night, she could not close her eyes, but during the day she walked outside with her baby, paying heed to different and mysterious sounds. They were talking to her, like letters of the alphabet. Putting them together, she could imagine all the happenings in their town. Sometimes, she could hear the terrifying quiet of the streets, interrupted only by sudden sounds of the local women weeping, lamenting their dead sons or husbands. She too often now cried for no tangible reasons. With her tears the pain slowly eased and a numbing cold congealed her heart.

"Weep, weeping dulls the inner pain." She remembered the words her mother used to tell her. And she cried, hearing the frightful sounds of war and the deadly quiet that scared her the most.

On that memorable day, the silent daybreak had been disturbed by remote lightning and some rare splashes of falling firebombs. It was one of those hot mornings at the beginning of September when the air was unusually sticky and muggy. Rebecca stepped outside, listening as always to the murmur of silence. The wind was talking to her, and the tree branches were touching her face. The grass, glistening with morning dew, petted her bare feet. And only the distant noise of those flying German warplanes and some remote explosions reminded her that the war was just around the corner. She went back to the house, put on her best dress, crimson red, swathed her baby in a light blanket and, pressing him to her heart, walked out of the house to the nearby wasteland.

The road to the wasteland was totally deserted, and only her lone figure was leaving a long, shimmering shadow on the sandy ground. She moved swiftly ahead as if trying to outstrip her own reflection. The yellow fireball of the sun dazzled her for a moment, and she lost her shadow. Now it lazily trudged after her, hiding and then suddenly appearing from behind the trees. Rebecca smiled—even her shadow was looking for shelter, afraid of the German warplanes, soaring loudly above her. And yet she stubbornly moved forward, acting impetuously, without thinking, as if she had lost her mind. There was madness in her eyes. Her loose, heavy hair swung in disarray across her shoulders, bathing in the generous sunlight. She felt dizzy. Suddenly, the sky, the earth and the trees—all revolved around her. She froze for a moment in the middle of the burnt land. The arms embracing her baby were raised to the sky. The German warplanes with black crosses on their wings glided low above her, so low that she could see the Nazis' pale, clean faces, and even the sleeves of their green uniforms.

Overcoming her giddiness, she trudged on further through the land, boldly flirting with death, begging the black beasts hovering above, to shoot her. And indeed, she didn't want to live anymore—she fell into a state of utter despair. The German warplanes continued to circle around her as she stubbornly and inexorably walked through the burning land, lamenting and begging them to kill her and her baby.

"Kill me, kill me," she shouted at the top of her lungs, "I

don't want to live."

Finally, totally exhausted, Rebecca sank to the ground, but still not a single shot had been heard. Before she collapsed, she saw a neighbor running towards her, waving her hands and trying to tell her something. It was the last thing she could remember.

The German pilots were amazed by such a mad Russian girl, walking through the burning land without any fear. Some locals, who saw the scene, angrily reported it to Igor.

"Keep your wife locked up. It looks like her mind is verging on madness. She is completely insane to behave like this now. Are there not already enough killings in our town? She is courting disaster and will bring it down upon us. After all, you shouldn't condone such behavior. For God sake, lock her up."

Igor was dismayed and frightened by Rebecca's actions. He returned home that night in a sullen mood and found Rebecca curled on the bed like a child, next to the crying baby. The red dress with the dirty spots on it lay on the floor. Igor knelt beside the bed.

"What has happened to you?" he asked her calmly, but she said nothing—only shot a quick, evasive look at him, utterly unconcerned.

Igor picked up the dress and put it on the bed next to her. She didn't move. He peered at her, patiently waiting for her reply, but her mind was still far away. Suddenly, she raised her head and glared at him with blurry, indifferent eyes.

"Igor, leave me alone. Go away. Please go away now."

Her behavior was totally incomprehensible to him. He stood there disoriented, not knowing what to do next, feeling her pain and her distress, and yet not being able to help. Finally, he turned around and stealthily glided out of the house.

The dark sky had descended on the roof of his house, and the evening haze had wrapped itself around the town, as if creating a wall between him and the world behind that wall. He groped his way through the darkness to the well, looking for the dip-bucket to get a drop of cold water. But not finding it, he fell heavily on the wet grass. Igor lay there quietly for a long time, realizing the full horror of their present circumstances and the ferocity of the world around him. At that moment, he knew that their young lives had been changed forever—there was no way back into the past, and death had become their only future....

* * * * *

Alex stopped talking and took a swallow of water. His throat was too dry to continue, and he was too depressed to talk. Eduardo kept silent. He needed time to comprehend the ferocity, the injustice and the horror of war, the inhumanity of human beings. But after a short pause, he asked the question that had been on his mind all the time while Alex was telling his story.

"Is Rebecca your mother?"

"I can't tell you right now," Alex ducked the question again. "We still have a long way to go. Look, Eduardo, why don't we take a walk to Central Park and continue talking? It's a beautiful day after all."

They left the restaurant still under the spell of Alex's story.

"Alex, I see you wear a wedding ring. Are you happy in your marriage?"

"I don't know what to tell you, Eduardo. Perhaps I am... but as for Eleanor..., my wife, I don't really know. She was my student before we got married. She was a very talented one."

They were about to sit on at the bench under a tree. Alex huddled up from the increasing wind.

"We should probably be going. I feel like having a cup of hot coffee again."

"That's a great idea. It's getting chilly." Eduardo agreed and continued questioning Alex. "Was Eleanor fascinated by your grandeur?"

Alex walked for some time, mulling over Eduardo's question.

"She was obsessed at the beginning. She needed me as her guide and her teacher. Eleanor is much younger than I."

"Is there a difference between love and obsession? Is it not true that obsession and love are identical emotional states?"

"Allow me to disagree with you, Eduardo. Love has positive energy—like the light or the sun—while obsession is dark, almost evil. Eleanor never loved me. I can say it now...but at that time....I believed she did. As for me, I loved her as I had never loved anybody before. After our marriage, I made several attempts to channel my emotions into my creative work. I dreamed of painting her portrait, a masterpiece that would make me famous. However, I could never paint a portrait of my wife the way I wished to depict her. The fact is that I failed to express strong emotions in the portrait, make the portrait talk, tell the story and simply to understand the woman I so passionately loved. Once, she disappeared from my life for a long time. It happened the day after our engagement, the day after I put a ring on her finger." Alex hesitated for a moment, debating whether to continue his story or not.

"Go on, Alex, you need to talk. I feel that there is a heavy burden on your soul. Please continue." Eduardo's voice was soft and encouraging.

Alex turned his head, watching a young, attractive woman pass by.

"Then, why you are still looking at other women?" Eduardo's voice expressed reproach.

Alex laughed. "It's a professional habit. I enjoy looking at beautiful things. I always have mistresses in spite of my feelings for my wife. She has recently grown too cold, too indifferent. You should understand that as an artist I need inspiration."

They walked into a coffee shop and found an empty table near a window. They both sank into silence, astonished by the bright sunlight coming through the window.

Some minutes passed before Alex continued his thought, "After things went wrong with Eleanor, I knew the only way to stifle my pain was to take a brush and through my work to plunge into another world, capture the innocent beauty of other women, who trusted me with their bodies and their souls. Strange isn't it?"

"No, it is not. I understand. At least, if you experienced real love once in your lifetime, you are a lucky man. It's a blessing. Do you think that Rebecca loved her husband?"

Alex mulled over the question for a couple of minutes, inhaling the aroma of strong coffee. He added three spoons of sugar, and slowly sipping from his cup, continued.

"She probably did love him at the beginning, but the war altered everything—people, their feelings, their views. Under extreme circumstances people change, and somehow everything bad or good comes to the surface. Not everyone can be strong when death follows your every step, when there is no guarantee that tomorrow you'll be still alive."

"Are you trying to justify Igor's behavior, Alex?"

"No, not at all, but to judge him you have to hear the whole story to the very end." Alex relaxed and looked at his watch. "It's almost two o'clock. I think I ought to finish my story about Rebecca and Igor."

"Did she too die at Blue Cottage?"

"Bear with me, Eduardo; I am coming to the end of my story about Rebecca and her husband. On that day, September fifth, Rebecca felt dizzy and completely worn out...."

Chapter Fourteen
Facing the Truth

*O*n that day, September fifth, Rebecca felt dizzy and completely worn out after the newborn baby had hardly slept the previous night, crying for milk she didn't have. Igor came home late. He tried now to be tender with his wife—she and his baby remained the only human beings he loved. His face and his clothes were covered with dust. There was a shattered look on his face. He embraced his wife and, crying like a child, told her what had really happened.

In the morning, Igor was ordered into the Gestapo's main office. The Gestapo was located in the old two-story building of the local bank. Walking down the empty streets, he felt that from now on disaster would always follow after him. He feared for Rebecca's life and his baby's, and ached not only for his own survival but also for the safety of his family. He owed it to his parents-in-law, to Rebecca.

He approached the familiar building and looked up. Red bricks embellished the entrance, and two angels with broken wings held the arch. The young German officer carefully checked his documents and took him upstairs. A lanky, young Nazi with a raw, but well-shaved face presided at the large table piled with papers. Puffing at his pipe, the officer contemptuously raked Igor with his small lackluster eyes and, goaded to fury by Igor's dithering, spoke in broken

Russian.

"So, I was told that you have a Jew in your house—in fact, two of them."

He pulled out the top folder and put it in front of him.

"Well, we have been patient with you long enough. It is my official obligation to give you a proper warning. It is time to get rid of them."

He then carefully leafed through the folder.

"I can see here that she is the daughter of a local rabbi. I heard that she is crazy anyway. Have you tried to pass her off as a Russian, you, idiot? She should be delivered to Blue Cottage immediately. Now!"

During his tirade, he gradually goaded himself into more fury.

"And you, yourself, should take her there. Do you hear my order? Now!" he screamed loudly in a pitched voice.

Igor cringed in horror—his mind was reeling. He tried hard to object, but it made the man even angrier.

"Shut up, I am not interested in your excuses. I am kind enough to spare your life...for now. It is an order. You can go. We are running out of time." He repeated his command, pointing at the door without glancing at Igor.

Igor left the building overwhelmed, not yet fully understanding that now on him and his family were simply doomed. Since that moment, time was moving inexorably toward the death of his family, toward the end of their young lives.

* * * * *

Half-an-hour later, Igor finished his story. Rebecca was silent but glared at him incredulously. She got up and for a minute stood in the middle of the room. She was lost in thought. Her mad eyes still had a weird expression of aloofness. Was she thinking about death and her baby, and wondering if it would be painful to die? She didn't fear death itself, and yet she knew that the pain of seeing her baby and her husband for the very last time would be unbearable. In silence, she docilely donned her jacket, comfortable shoes, tied back her thick hair with a red ribbon and looked at her husband.

"It's time to go, Igor. Don't cry. It won't help. I am ready. You can take me to Blue Cottage. I am not afraid to share my fate with my friends and relatives," she said calmly without a hint of fear.

"Please, Rebecca, please listen to me, we still have one last chance to escape, to find the resistance group. Let's do it now, hurry up, Rebecca."

His voice became imploring. He lurched and flailed about the room in a state of total disarray, trying to convince Rebecca to run away.

"No, Igor, it's impossible. If the resistance group finds you, they'll kill you as a traitor, and they may not spare the life of our baby. If I escape with the baby, the Gestapo will not spare your life, and it's not sure that I will be welcomed by partisans. You heard the stories too how many Jews have been executed by their own so-called fellow countrymen. I don't want to jeopardize your life or our baby's. At least now, there is a chance to save you and Alek. Take him to the nearby church. I heard that the priest is hiding some Jewish children there."

"I won't let you go. I won't let you die!!!" Igor lost his temper as he continued to scurry about the room, like a caged wounded animal.

Rebecca watched him almost indifferently without saying a word. She knew how much he was suffering, but she remained deaf to his entreaties.

Finally, Igor put his head down and gave up. "You won this time, Rebecca. I have to save our child. I understand."

He stared at his wife as if trying to memorize her every feature. And then, he wrapped his arms around her. He remained motionless for a long time. She caressed his hair until finally she forced him to get up. He could not stop and continued quietly lamenting, still not being able to accept the inevitable.

"They will answer with their lives for what they have done to our country, to my family. What evil power led me to believe them? One day, I'll take vengeance on the enemy. I promise, Rebecca, I promise. I know now that I committed an unforgivable sin. Forgive me, Rebecca. Forgive me, my love."

Frantic with grief, he took his crying son into his arms.

"Get those loony ideas out of your head, Igor. Don't blame yourself—it's not your fault that instead of love hatred grew in your heart when the evil Bolshevik regime took away your parents' lives. And don't act recklessly, Igor, please. You have to take care of Alek. Remember?"

He gradually acquiesced, realizing that he was only causing more pain for Rebecca. As the night fell, they prayed together. Igor held the Holy Scriptures in his hands and swore to Rebecca that he would take care of their son. Finally, after long prayers, they took refuge in each other arms, forgetting for a moment of tomorrow and fear of the coming end.

The last flash of hope petered out as hand in hand they walked out into the enshrouding darkness of the night.... Igor carefully pressed the baby to his heart. A little wisp of a cold black moon waded through the heavy clouds. The vagrant flux of light was dispersed all over the sky. *Yesterday, today and tomorrow, every night, in spite of war and suffering, and all the ruins, above all of these, the moon will always shine in the dark universe, illuminating a path to the future,* Rebecca thought, walking away from her life.

Chapter Fifteen
The Execution

*A*t dawn, on September 7th, Igor witnessed how Blue Cottage hosted the first mass execution of men, women and children. The crowd of about 80 men was rounded up at a desolate field, not far from the railroad station. The whole scene looked totally surreal. They stood tightly pressed to each other. The first sunbeams threw a yellow light on their haggard faces. Igor was in the hordes with other local policemen. First, they called out all the men and ordered to dig a deep grave. Like in a dreadful dream, they pushed the men to the edge and forced them to jump.

Only one young Jewish boy, about sixteen years old, tried to resist, screaming at the top of his lungs, "Я ненавижу вас всех, фашисты, убийцы."[4] His cry outraged the German officer. His face turned red as he seethed with anger. The Nazi spun around and with a powerful blow repeatedly hit the boy with the butt of his gun. The boy lost balance and fell to the ground, frantically and stubbornly repeating the same words, spitting out a curse upon his murderers.

"Фашисты, убийцы! Фашисты, убийцы! Я ненавижу вас всех. Будьте вы все прокляты!"[5]

---

[4] I hate you all, fascists, murders. (translated from Russian)

[5] Fascists, murders, fascists, murders. Confound you all! (translated from Russian)

The officer threw a withering look at the boy. "I'll teach you, you Jewish swine," he screamed and, fiddling with his gun, began shooting until a bullet went through the boy's heart.

Igor closed his eyes, veered quickly to one side and stopped, as if turned to stone—he couldn't kill these young men, women and children. He felt terribly dizzy. A cold thrill of horror passed through his body. When at last he opened his eyes, it was all over. The dead, along with the wounded, were huddled together. The grave moved, breathing, while the policemen threw earth on bodies, dead or alive. The rest dissolved in Igor's memory. Later, he couldn't recall any events of that horrific day.

On the early afternoon of the same day, after the Nazis had gotten rid of all the Jewish men, the last group of approximately 800 women and children, doomed to die, under the protection of the SS, huddled together awaiting their fate. A Russian policeman ordered every woman and child to strip naked, except for a few old women, who had to expose only the upper part of their bodies. All the women lamented and refused to undress, trying to hold on to their children, not letting them go. The murderers were furious and did their best to make sure that every child was separated from his or her mother. Soon, after all the children were winnowed from their mothers, there was the order given to kill the children first. The children cried loudly, fiercely resisting the Nazis, helplessly pressing their shaking bodies to their mothers.

The execution lasted all day long, even after the red ball of sun had vanished beyond the horizon. The whole scene had sunk into obscurity. Under the pall of the abysmal night, one of the women darted into the woods but was caught. She was pushed on to her knees, and in front of the crowd she was mercilessly pummeled. The German officer struck her with a long whip again and again. She let out a squeal and fell silent. It maddened him, and he struck her again with all his might, though not a pant escaped from her anymore. Her courage threw him into a rage, and he continued beating her ruthlessly until her blood covered his clean, polished boots. He took a snow-white handkerchief from his pocket and carefully wiped off his boots. Only then, being sure she was dead, he ordered a policeman to haul her body down onto the cliff.

From the steep angle of her vision Rebecca saw the whole scene, when in the flash of the light she recognized the woman's face—it was her birth mother. A scream curdled in her throat. Instantly, Rebecca remembered her mother's last words: "We are two strangers on a train heading to nowhere, or…perhaps…to our demise. We are all going to die, all of us, but before I did hope you would be able to find in your heart compassion and forgiveness…."

"I forgive you, mama. I forgive…." Rebecca whispered into the air, but it was too late—the woman could no longer hear her words. A hush fell over the crowd. Somebody grabbed Rebecca by the hand. She turned around and recognized her cousin, Roza.

"Be brave, Rebecca. God will take us to heaven," Roza said quietly into her ear but abruptly stopped, when one of the fascists, with big glasses on his red round face, laid his eyes on Rebecca.

"How did you get here? You don't look like a Jew." He gazed devouringly at her, raking her slender body with his bestial eyes. "You are a beautiful girl, and I could definitely find a good use for you in my household."

He bared his teeth in an insensate grimace, stroking Rebecca's naked arms and patting her on the back. She followed the words that leapt from his mouth like noisy black flies. As these dirty flies flew into the pitch dark to their freedom, her face turned ghastly pale.

"I am a Jew, and I am proud to be a Jew." Rebecca spieled off, trying to enunciate every word clearly, watching him with disdain. At this moment, she had no fear, no despair. She only felt tremendously sad that her short life was going to end right now, and she bravely waited for that moment to happen.

The man's eyebrows rose in astonishment. "I'll make you pay, you Jewish bastard," he cursed with malicious joy, while his face turned purple with rage, and the red pimples on his forehead were about to explode. "I'll make you pay," he repeated loudly and hit her across the face. And with one ample swoop he pushed her into the ditch on top of the other still alive bodies and shot her in the head.

Then he turned to Roza and pulled her out. "You'll go with me. Are you also a Jew?"

Roza didn't deign him an answer, but instead she looked around, as if searching for help and then with all her might spat into his face.

"I am a man of a facetious temper!!!" The Nazi screamed and wiped it off with disgust. Then he drew himself up to his full height and pushed her further into the woods. A short time later, they heard Roza's long and helpless screams and then some gunshots, and everything suddenly merged into a long, horrific silence. Upon finishing his odious business, the Nazi showed up again, buttoning his pants on the move. Just in a little more than two weeks Roza would have turned eighteen years old.

At his order, a few SS men hurriedly threw the remaining victims into the ditch and shot them all from above. The ceaseless, heart-rending cries pierced the air for a long time after the execution. The mound breathed and moved all night long after the SS and policemen had left the murderous scene. For the next three days, the local people could hear groans and cries from the grave but were afraid to approach. Altogether, 2,000 Nevel Jews perished at Blue Cottage. Rebecca was among them.

With time, their bodies turned into grains of dust that mantled the trees, the grass and the wild flowers growing at the foot of the mass grave. The next day, early in the morning, Igor came to the pit. It was now covered with earth and heaps of small stones. It seemed to him that the mound of earth and the hillock of grass around it were still heavily breathing and loudly groaning. On top of it, he found a red ribbon. It was all that was left of his wife.

* * * * *

Upon finishing his story, Alex too felt emotionally exhaustted, but after a long, seemingly interminable silence, he continued, "It makes my blood crawl when I think about the Nazi atrocities. During the years of the German occupation, 24,000 thousands of Nevel's citizens had been tortured and shot to death. Nearly 10,000 had been taken for penal servitude to the Nazi labor camps in Germany, and nearly 150 villages had been destroyed and burned. Only on October 6th, 1943, did the Red Army begin the liberation of Nevel." He paused. "Actually, did you notice today's date?"

"October 6, 2003. I see your point—today is the anniversary. The liberation of Nevel began exactly sixty years ago. What an awful fate! Have you ever visited that town?"

"No, I haven't, but, in fact, my father did. He visited Blue Cottage, and there was a monument erected at the foot of the grave. Rebecca's name is engraved among those who perished there."

"Alex, you promised to tell me what happened to Igor." Eduardo tilted back in his chair.

"Well, it is difficult to talk about it, even after so many years have gone by, but you need to know his fate. Here it goes....The first days of autumn fell on earth with a deluge of rain....".

Chapter Sixteen
The Madman

*T*he first days of autumn fell on earth with a deluge of rain and lonely, gloomy nights. Now the cold rays of sun poured down only rarely on earth.

After Rebecca's execution, sleep totally evaded Igor. Restless, he passed most of the night near his crying baby. Bewildered by the recent events, he couldn't forgive himself for the tragic and calamitous mistake he had made in joining the Nazis, or for the disillusionment that had blighted the end of Rebecca's life. He eventually arrived at the conclusion that the German Army invaded Russia not to free millions of her people from the power of Bolshevism but to enslave them and destroy their motherland. They came not to fight the oppressive Soviet system but to fight the oppressed. On the one hand, there was Hitler, a monstrous murderer, but on the other hand, there was their own murderer of innocent people, Joseph Stalin....

After these reflections, he was confused and began to loath every minute of his existence. The only purpose of his life was his son, but Igor was afraid to keep Alek at home, knowing that he too would be taken away from him. On a cold, rainy morning, following Rebecca's advice, he wrapped his son in a warm blanket, tied with his wife's red ribbon and took him to the nearby church, the only church that had not yet been destroyed.

The next day, at dawn, with a jittery feeling, Igor stared out of the window. The horrific scene paralyzed him for a moment. The sky was ablaze with a mass of flame—the church was consumed by fire. The Nazis, suspecting that the priest was hiding Jewish children in his church, had set it on fire.

Instantly, on the verge of madness, Igor raced out of the house. "The church...the church is on fire. My son...my son...," he screamed and ran as fast as he could until he reached the old building and saw that it had been burnt down to the ground.

The lurid reflection of the blazing flames covered the sky, casting an ominous shadow on the debris. A German officer watched the flames with pleasure, holding in his hands an old Russian sacred icon, a Mother and Child. The bodies of the local priest and his wife had been burned beyond any recognition.

Like a madman pushed to his limits, Igor circled around the church, looking for his son, digging deep into the ashes, the shattered glass, broken into shards, burnt furniture, trying to stamp out the fire until his hands were all covered with blood. A suffocating smell of human flesh caused him to stop searching and turned his emotions into scalding anguish.

Only late at night did he return home. He lay down, hoping to get some sleep, but he was kept awake by fitful dreams in which visions of familiar faces looked at him reproachfully from the grave. His life had lost all savor and no longer had any meaning. He felt as if his hands were steeped in the blood of those he loved. He jumped up and looked at his hands—blood was trickling down onto his underwear. Horrified, in a state of near insanity, Igor grabbed his gun and, hastily pulling on his trousers, rushed down the stairs and out of the house.

A full round moon shone down from a sky studded with

small, scintillating stars. The world seemed to be peaceful and quiet, as if the earth had forgotten the war, death, all the suffering and murders. Igor staggered grief-stricken around the house and then, like a wild animal, set off down the path to the woods, looking for a shelter from his madness. A strong wind blew relentlessly into his face, shaking the brittle tree branches damaged by the war. Falling to the ground, they rattled under his feet, and in the rustling sound of the leaves he heard voices, calling for him, screaming for help. He looked up at the moon, now hardly discernible, obscured by heavy clouds, and through these passing clouds he saw images and heard the loud sobbing of those who had been murdered at Blue Cottage. His eyes, wide-open, looked farther, searching for the familiar face of his wife among the crowd that was condemned to die. Rebecca was there, gazing at him in agony with a faint smile on her lips. And then, her image slowly glided away into the dark depths of the universe.

Running blindly through the woods, Igor darted down to the river, trying to escape the images, the horror, the voices. A carrion-crow, prophet of evil, shot up into the sky. Startled, Igor followed the trajectory of the bird's flight until it disappeared from view. He took it for a bad omen, seeing himself lost in a labyrinth without end. He began to walk faster and faster along the edge of a formidable rock precipice. As he ran on and on, his madness gradually subsided and turned into anger at himself, at Rebecca, at the whole world.

Shortly afterwards, the river turned sharply in a bend, and the bank began its oblique ascent. He glanced up and saw how the ominous reflection of the flames from the burning church hung in the sky, leaving a narrow red path on the smooth surface of the riverbed, where it merged with the earth and turned into one dark grave. He fell to his knees and begged God to grant him absolution from his sins, and then, for the last time, he looked up at the moon, as if saying good-bye to Rebecca, and put the gun to his temple....

His body slithered down the steep bank and, tumbling into the abyss, became light as a feather, until the dark water closed above him.

* * * * *

"During the years of the German occupation, 1,032 Jewish boys and girls volunteered to go to war to defend their country. It was only on October sixth, 1943, that the Red Army liberated Nevel, by that time dashed to pieces," Alex finished his narration.

Eduardo seemed to be in shock. Then, looking about, as if to make sure nobody could hear him, he began talking:

"The war, the destruction—to me it is the end of civilization. Why did the world tolerate the madness of Hitler or of Stalin? It was as if the world closed its eyes to murder, criminal acts and the extermination of a whole nation. I loathe such passivity, indifference, when terrorists are throwing bombs, killing people, and the earth is set on fire. What a horrific fate. It's hard to comprehend all of this."

He paused and glanced questioning at Alex who immediately responded:

"Actually, I feel the same way, but it is enough for now. Let's meet for dinner at six at the same restaurant again. We still have about two hours for a nap. I'll tell you what happened next. Agreed?"

Chapter Seventeen

Lost Hope

*E*duardo returned to his hotel room and lay down, feeling an immense sadness. Thoughts of Rebecca, Igor and their baby pulled him into a deep, depressive mood. How could he be related to these people and to Alex? Or was he? And yet, with all his intuition, he felt that he and Alex were like brothers, kindred spirits. He hoped that they were related, but he still couldn't imagine any tangible connections. Rarely in his busy life had he allowed himself to ruminate over the past. However, this unexpected encounter with Alex turned his life upside down.

Although Eduardo lived by impulse, accepting each moment as it came, only his music and art were permanent in his life. Upon his return to Italy from that memorable trip, he felt suddenly incomplete, lost, lonely. He saw Nora's image everywhere he went, in every woman he met. His fame didn't bring him happiness—something was still missing in his life, and this missing part was—love.

And yet, looking now deep down inside his soul, he realized that it was Nora who inspired him to find the meaning of life and to rediscover his art. He learned anew that to live meant to express your inner feelings and emotions in creativity, to go beyond the boundaries, and not only to create art, but in the process to rediscover your own soul. It seemed to him that everything he had previously done or lived for had been a lie, and that only now he found the truth, the real meaning of his existence.

Probably Alex's story had stirred up Eduardo's own old memories. The rest of the afternoon he mused fitfully, trying to remember details of Alex's story and to find a path to his own past.

* * * * *

In the evening, the weather worsened, and an autumn drizzle fell upon the earth like a thin, lacey tunic. Eduardo took a walk around the hotel and only then went to the restaurant to meet Alex. The streets were crowded, but he hardly saw the people around him. He could still imagine those innocents who perished from the surface of the earth through the cruelty of Nazis. Eduardo entered to the restaurant earlier, way before six, so he had enough time to order a drink. To his surprise, Alex appeared on time, looking suddenly aged and tired.

"I need a drink." He sat down heavily across from Eduardo.

"You looked better in the morning. What happened to you? Did you have a nap? Actually, I have already ordered drinks. What would you like for dinner?"

"I'll have the same. I guess we have the same taste in many things. Don't we?"

"Then, it's a deal." Eduardo placed the order and turned back to his previous question. "So, what happened? Did you get some sleep?"

"No, not really. I had time to think about things that I had scarcely thought about before we met. Look, Eduardo, I have to be brief. My wife will be arriving tomorrow morning, right before the opening of the exhibition. I want to finish my story. We are still far from solving our mystery, although I see such an unusual interlocking of events. Where did we stop?"

A dark shadow crossed his face. He looked as if his thoughts were in disarray, but he began his narration: "On October the sixth, 1943, the Russian Army, along with local guerillas, went on the offensive...."

* * * * *

On October the sixth, 1943, the Russian Army along with local guerillas went on the offensive for the liberation of Nevel. In spite of fierce resistance from the German Army, it took only five days to scour all the invaders from the land. A sweeping and full-scale offensive of the Russian Army allowed it in a short time to destroy the powerful German fortifications and unexpectedly to take Nevel back from the Nazis. The Nevel operation of October 6 – October 10, 1943, had been one of the briefest offensives of the war, but the heavy battles for the total liberation of Nevel from the Germans lasted until January of 1944.

During that time, the German Army, in a panic, packed up everything they could carry and hastily scurried away from the town. Along the way, they drove the young people, men and women out of the villages to work in forced labor camps in Germany. Strangely enough, some locals and peasants from the surrounding villages willingly joined the Nazis.

Fear, horror of the unknown and anxiety drove people from their homes. A growing crowd of people, hungry, dust-covered and ragged, stretched out along the muddy roads, moving together in confluent streams. Everyone had their own reasons to leave: some feared to stay because they had been helping the SS to get rid of Jews and communists, but some were leaving because they hated the Soviet regime and were afraid of its oppression.

A panic seized the people as a long procession dragged out along Vitebsk Avenue. In a sense, it was similar to the procession of Jewish people walking to their execution only a short while ago. Exhausted and frustrated, the crowd moved farther and farther from their homes. There were many sick and wounded among them, but they had no medications or medical help. The villages they passed seemed to be deserted. The windows and doors were shut, and only hungry stray dogs and cats wandered around looking for food. The cold stars, like small fireflies, twinkled in the distant sky as the crowd walked calmly down the dirty road to their unknown fate.

Meanwhile, other inhabitants began to return to their demolished homes and utterly changed landscape. Little by little, the town was coming back to life. The burning cars with the German swastika were still there, and some buildings still carried signs written in German. Torn posters, proclaimming German victory, were scattered about the streets, and local people walked on them indifferently. The bridge over the river Emenka had been destroyed and was sadly reminiscent of a lamenting creature falling to its knees. Still burning German tanks lay on their sides in ominous positions, like huge black spiders protruding from the surface of the river.

In the middle of the square, famously named after Karl Marx, his grandiose statue had been completely demolished, and his huge head with the curly beard now rested at the foot of the pedestal, a powerful symbol of the destruction and folly of war.

Out of the ashes, the town began the mysterious process of rebuilding, and its inhabitants lived now with a timid feeling of hope.

* * * * *

The following summer, after a long and enervating trip, Eliza and Samuel returned to their home, hoping against hope to find Rebecca and a message from their sons.

They arrived on foot late in the day. Through the dusk, they could see the welter of ruined buildings which, uprooted from their soil, had become merely a pile of loose stones. Only the vestiges of a few houses and the walls of their small synagogue still remained untouched. The city looked devastated, dingy and drab, like a human being, who after enduring great suffering, was only now on the way to recovery. A brisk wind scattered and swirled pieces of debris all over their narrow street.

Eliza and Samuel knew nothing about Rebecca's fate and were looking forward to seeing her and their grandchild, but they saw no signs of a living soul, no word of them. Their house looked so lonesome near the old cemetery amidst the debris of their ruined hopes. The windows were nailed shut with plywood. The wild flowers bent their blooms down close to the ground, as if deep sorrow had pressed them down to earth.

Samuel inserted his old key into the rusted keyhole. As he turned the key, it produced a mournful sound. He had to push the door hard before managing to open it. They crept into their dark dwelling and froze on the threshold. The dirty windows had been boarded up, and the feeble light could scarcely filter through them. They stood at the doorway as agonizing memories of their last days there rushed back. They heard the voices of their loved ones, felt their presence in the room but did not recognize the once familiar place.

Although the house was empty, it was a total shambles, as if the war had tried to destroy everything that belonged to their past. The mirror, dangling awry, was coated with a thick layer of dust and had a crack right in the middle. The old cuckoo clock on the wall had frozen in the past, no longer ticking but staring at them, trying to reveal a deep secret, hidden behind the walls of this abandoned house. A pail, full of dead water, drawn from the well, stood in the kitchen, spreading a dank and acrid odor of mold. It felt as if life had deserted this house long time ago. During their absence, not only they, but their cozy, little house had grown older, darker and grimier. The scene made Eliza nauseated and brought her sheer misery. She stepped outside, unable to comprehend what she had just seen.

"There is going to be a thunderstorm," she muttered in a colorless voice, gulping back her tears. She sank heavily onto the steps, struggling to quell a sense of loss such as she had never experienced before.

And indeed, from far away, a burst of thunder rocked the sky, and a slanting murk of rain fell upon the earth. Through the wall of rain, she saw the fast approaching night. And she sensed with growing dread the inevitability of what they were about to learn. With her mother's heart, Eliza suddenly realized that this heavy rainfall was washing out her last hope of being reunited with her children.

That same evening, after the thunder had rumbled away, the sky finally cleared up from the low floating clouds. Eliza and Samuel sat on the steps of their house, pondering their future. Eliza leaned against her husband's shoulder, and he heard the loud beating of her heart.

"We have to start our lives all over again. We have to stay alive to find our children. We can't just sit here doing nothing. I can't be at peace with myself until I know what has happened to them."

Her calm words swayed in the breeze, leaving only a tiny echo in the tree branches. Samuel put his arm around his wife's shoulders. Her pain interlocked and echoed with his own pain, and his own grief. They wanted to wake up from their horrific nightmare, to return to their happy past, as if the war and murder of innocent people had never taken place on this earth.

One week passed before they found out what had happened to their daughter and son-in-law. They also tried to find the whereabouts of Alek, their grandchild, but all their efforts led nowhere. They went from house to house, looking for someone who could tell them about the fate of their family. Some people were friendly, others didn't want to talk.

At the end of the week, as night fell heavily over the town, they heard a cautious knock at the door. It was their neighbor, an old Jewish woman, whose whole family had been executed at Blue Cottage, but she had miraculously escaped, hiding in the cold basement of her house, until she learned that the German troops had left town. She would go outside late at night and search cautiously around for food and water. On one of those nights, she saw with her own eyes the burning church and Igor's mad race toward death. As for the child, she heard that he had died during the church fire. That's all she could tell.

Countless times Eliza walked numbly through the city to Blue Cottage. The mass grave was now heavily covered with tall grass and wild flowers. She would bring fresh-cut flowers and put them at the foot of the grave. The red blooms of poppies were scattered around like bloodstains of those who had been murdered there. And yet, for Eliza it became such a peaceful place—a place of seclusion. Bent over with sorrow, she spent days sitting alone near the mound, talking to Rebecca and to others who had perished there. On windy days, she heard their voices, and she cried, thanking God for giving her a chance to talk to her daughter and to ask her forgiveness.

Returning home, she would walk along the river, unable to recognize the beauty of her beloved landscape. At a slow pace, like a ghost, she roamed stealthily about the familiar places, moving away from the chanting melody of the dark river that looped along the banks, the same river that had swallowed up so many innocent lives, including her son-in-law. The lull of its dark waters, carrying the mystery of human tragedy, was maddening for Eliza.

As for Samuel, he passed most of his time rebuilding their house, reading and praying. He too could not get out of his head the execution of Nevel's Jews, the untimely death of Rebecca and Igor's suicide. Now, his memories often returned to the past, questioning his decision to leave Rebecca. He wished he had stayed and shared the fate of the others—he found it meaningless to go on living like that. The only light in his aimless existence were his sons and the hope to see them again one day.

A month after they had settled in their house, a strange letter arrived from Leon. It was a short message dated June, 1942. He wrote that they were both fine and were looking forward to the victorious end of the war. This small note bolstered some of their lost hopes.

Chapter Eighteen
A Beggar-woman

*T*wo months after their return, they heard rumors that a woman—a stranger to the town, with a small child, had been wandering aimlessly through the streets, begging for food and water. It was wartime, everything around them had been destroyed. The Nazis were nearby and Stalin was in power. People were afraid of their own shadows. There were virtually no men left in town. Winter that year happened to be extremely rigorous, with an abundance of hail, sleet and snow.

One night, the hail turned into a heavy snowfall. The wind blew in great gusts, and its shrieks reminded of the loud wailing of untamed beasts. The wind fiercely shook the windowpanes, broke the tree branches. Piles of snow blanketed all the roads, like clean white bandages on the bleeding wounds of the earth. Benumbed with cold, a bedraggled woman dressed in rags, with a child in her arms, walked blindly through the deserted streets, asking for food and shelter. Wrapped in her torn, filthy clothes, she looked like a beggar.

It was already after midnight, and a heavy hail was knocking on the roofs of the houses along with a wailing northern wind. In this weather the stranger reached Eliza's house. They were not yet asleep. Eliza was cleaning the kitchen, and Samuel was reading the Torah aloud when they heard a feeble knock at the door. For a moment, Samuel was seized by sudden fear, but then he thought about his sons and rushed to open the door.

A smile of gratitude radiated across the woman's peaked and pallid face when Samuel opened the door to her. Shivering with cold, the woman with a child in her arms stopped on the threshold in doubt. Their dirty tattered clothes were covered with ice and snow. The child, a boy with a haggard face, who was about a year old, looked scared and exhaustted, and yet he didn't cry. His eyes were closed, and his face was deadly pale. In spite of her dirty clothes and wan look, the woman appeared to be very young and beautiful. Great sadness and deep suffering emanated from her expressive, dark hazel eyes.

"Please come in. It's too cold to stand in the doorway."

Samuel took the child and gave him to Eliza. He rubbed the woman's hands in his. They were so cold that she could hardly move her fingers.

"You are so kind to me, but honestly, I am fine...just my son." Her quiet words melted in the air like small snowflakes.

"You can go to the kitchen, dear, while my wife heats a bath for you and your child, and then we will have supper. Don't be afraid. We live alone, far from other houses, and will be happy to help you."

He saw that she was about to faint and, gently taking her by the hand, led the woman to the kitchen for a glass of hot tea.

After having a bath and getting clean clothes that had belonged to Rebecca, the woman appeared in the dining room. Her wet, raven-black, curly hair spread out over her shoulders, and her small delicate features revealed her noble origin. There was a maidenly innocence and modesty about her, and yet something very magnetic and tragic in the way she looked and walked. She said that she was not hungry and asked only for a cup of hot milk and a piece of dry bread for her son and herself.

Upon finishing her supper, the woman put her son to bed and sat quietly by the window, peering through it at the mound of earth, buried in the pure whiteness. She cried soundlessly and seemed to be remote and shy. No one knew why she was crying, but it was easy to see from her sad eyes and deep circles under them that she had suffered immensely. Feeling her grief, Eliza and Samuel did not ask her any questions. In fact, Eliza made a bed for her and her child in the same room where Rebecca used to sleep and then brought out their old album, full of family photos, in order to make the woman feel comfortable, like a part of their family. The woman was extremely touched by their kindness and, wiping her tears, warmly embraced Eliza. She then sat down at the table with the family to look at the old photographs.

* * * * *

Alex stopped talking, cleared his throat and sipped some wine.

Eduardo hung upon every word, attempting to comprehend the story and make sense of it. Suddenly, it crossed his mind to ask: "Was the woman a soothsayer?"

"Well, actually, I have not finished. She was not. I heard this story from my father many times, and every time it gave me a chill. I had hoped that one day I would be able to unravel the mystery of that woman, who had changed our lives, but events turned differently. The mystery was untangled by itself, unexpectedly....Look, Eduardo, we are both swept by emotion. It's getting late. Why not save the rest of our story for tomorrow? I'll continue it at breakfast and tell you all I know about this mysterious woman."

Chapter Nineteen
A Sleepless Night

*I*t was almost midnight, but Alex still tossed restlessly in bed from side to side. Several times he drifted into somnolence but was awakened by queer images. He was thinking about his life devoted to art, women that often appeared in his life and easily disappeared without leaving any impresssion. For a long time, he lay in bed sleepless, submerged in the depth of his thoughts, trying to get rid of unimportant ones and to hold on to the important events of his life, as though he wanted to see the whole picture, not just some small and insignificant fragments. Still, the whole picture fell apart; some parts of the chain were missing, the most needed ones. He wanted to dredge up memories of his relationship with Eleanor—the story of their love affair, but could not remember anything special. For him, their love story consisted of stormy emotions, ascents and descents, prolonged conversations, deep understanding and stubborn misunderstanding, the complete, merging of their souls, and then long and painful disconnection.

Eleanor was his student, a strange girl with absentminded, inscrutable eyes, usually gliding from one face to another, as if she were blind or perfectly absorbed in her inner world. Nevertheless, she listened to his lectures hungrily devouring his every word.

* * * * *

He well remembered the day he first noticed Eleanor in the front row of the auditorium. Alex carefully scanned the overcrowded hall, stepped out from the podium and began to pace back and forth, mentally preparing for his lecture.

Meanwhile, the girl scrutinized him closely, exchanging words with her friend. He watched her from the corner of his eye. Approaching her bench, he noticed that the girl had made a sharp drawing of his face. He thought that in this pencil sketch he had quite a devilish expression and looked older than in real life. She saw a sign of disappointment on his face and began to examine him again. Alex knew he looked much younger than his forties, being athletically built, broad-shouldered, with keen, green-blue eyes, burning with curiosity. He had refined, expressive features and an oval-shaped face with no wrinkles. His chin bore signs of stubbornness and a strong will. His hair had barely noticeable touches of gray at the temples. His curly, masterly clipped beard was totally gray, and that probably revealed his age. In Eleanor's drawing of him, he looked very attractive, but at the same time he saw something very unappealing or perhaps even unpleasant in his appearance.

Being totally absorbed in her sketch, Eleanor no longer paid any attention to him. Professor Gold smiled sarcastically at such an unflattering portrait and began his lecture as always with a question addressed directly to his audience.

"I've just noticed there are some talented artists in our audience," he said with a furtive smile, "and I'd like them to answer my question. Can you compare the birth of a painting with the birth of a child?" He looked at Eleanor, who at that very moment put down her pencil, and was seemingly revved up.

His strong deep voice immediately affected his other students. For some time, a total silence wrapped the auditorium. Alex looked around and repeated his question again.

"I want to know your opinion if we can compare the birth

of a painting with the birth of a child?"

At once, all of them began talking, interrupting one another. Alex waited patiently, allowing them to express their thoughts, and then lifted his hand, signaling for them to be quiet. Gradually, the audience became silent again, and he continued, trying to avoid Eleanor's persistent gaze.

"The history of every single painting is no less mysteryous or interesting than the life of an artist himself. I hope you agree with me." He went back to the podium.

"In my opinion, the birth of a painting can easily be compared with the birth of a child. Every painting comes into the world through the creative and painful agony of the artist. His creative impetus, his talent, his genius, the ascent of his spirit do not disappear but are transmuted into his work—his child—and remain there for centuries, for the lifetime of his creation in order to make his work eternal and his name unforgettable. The creative energy he applies to his work lives forever. The process of creativity itself is so incredibly complicated. With every movement of his brush and its every stroke, a new portrait is born. We can feel the heart beating, the blood flowing through the veins of his sitters. A new face is captured forever in a heavy golden frame. Whose heart is beating under the silk and velvet draperies of those luxurious clothes? Is it the heart of a courtesan, a famous actress, a gentleman or it is the heart of the artist himself, who invested his own life in every marvel that he has created?"

Alex paused and then continued, "During his nine years at the court of Charles I, Anthony Van Dyck executed more than thirty portraits of the English King, and three-hundred-fifty portraits of his noble attendees. Van Dyck died at the age of forty-three. The rumors spread that he died from extensive drinking and numerous love affairs."

Alex stopped talking for a minute to let the information sink in and glanced at Eleanor. She listened to him with her eyes closed, as if she were dreaming. At that very moment, she thought that he could probably enliven any subject of his lecture with his passionate discourse. He approached her and continued his thoughts, addressing them to her only.

"To be precise, his title of court painter demanded highly intensive and constant labor. He longed to depict nature, to isolate himself from rich society life. His weary soul yearned for the peace and quietude that he could find only in nature. In my opinion, he died from selling his soul to the devil. Yes, that's exactly what I mean."

He noticed that Eleanor opened her eyes and stared at him, obviously puzzled. He began to pace between the rows, disturbed by her intense gaze.

"Later, when we'll talk about his early work, you will be able to understand what I really mean by this statement. Painting portraits of the rich and famous exhausted him physically and spiritually. His dreams crashed. His soul died. He burned himself in his own unsatisfied fervor. It's interesting to note that his subtle psychological and deep insight into the souls of his models had a dramatic effect on his portraits as if he had foreseen their tragic end, including the portraits of the English King, Charles I, himself, who was doomed to die at the guillotine. Later on, the same qualities of sensitive understanding of his sitter's souls were evident in portraits of the Italian artist Amadeus Modigliani and the Russian painter Valentine Serov. I would like to cite the words of the French writer Honoré de Balzac: 'He touched the sky while walking firmly on earth.'"

Alex's voice wobbled, and he surveyed the auditorium until he met again the same attentive eyes of the girl in the first row. She didn't avert her gaze and continued staring at him while thinking about his statement.

He closed his notes and went to the screen to illustrate his point of view with some slides.

* * * * *

What did he do wrong? Why did he have such an unhappy marriage, distant relations with his wife? Was it the differ-

ence in their age? She blamed him for the distance between them, his coldness and that he could not give her a child. She criticized his art for not being profound enough, and that he was selling his talent for money. She even tried to compare him to Van Dyck.

Alex curled up under the blanket, closed his eyes, and slowly his dreams faded away. Somnolence fogged his memory, and just before daybreak he was soundly engulfed in slumber. A different dream, painted in bright colors, appeared in his imagination—distorted faces laughing at him, like images from the Peter Brueghel painting, hung in his living room.

It was almost eight-thirty when he opened his eyes, feeling completely washed out by his strange dream. He tried to remember Freud's interpretation of dreams but could not come up with any explanation.

Chapter Twenty
Family Album

*W*hen Alex walked into the restaurant, Eduardo was already there drinking his coffee.

"Good morning, Eduardo," he greeted him like an old friend.

"Good morning, Alex. You're late, and I'm quite impatient as you can guess." His eyes shone with excitement. "I have already ordered your favorite pancakes with strawberry jam."

Alex called the waiter and continued. "Sorry to be late. Bad dreams disturbed my sleep as always nowadays. I thought about my wife and our first trip to Washington."

"It was probably a pleasant reminiscence. Why do you call it a bad dream?"

"It is hard to explain. Perhaps…some other time." His face darkened, and Eduardo didn't proceed with his inquires.

"What about you? Did you have peaceful dreams last night?"

"I couldn't sleep well, thinking about Rebecca, Igor and the fate of those who were so mercilessly murdered at Blue Cottage. Who was that young woman with a child? Do you know anything about her? You left me puzzled yesterday. I need to know what came next." Eduardo stared at Alex questioningly, anxious to hear the rest of the story.

"Let me just wait until this coffee wakes me up completely, so I can concentrate on what I am about to tell you. It's important."

Alex swallowed his last pancake, finished his coffee and kept silent for some time, trying to pull together his scattered thoughts. After some hesitation, he returned to the narrative he had been forced to interrupt the previous evening.

"So, Eliza showed this woman their family album...."

* * * * *

Eliza showed the woman their family album. She sat next to her, leafing through the pages of the thick book. The woman looked at the old photographs with tremendous curiosity, poring carefully over every picture until she stumbled across some photographs of the twin brothers just before they went to war. She lifted the album to her eyes, as if not believing what she saw and then, suddenly closing it, she darted a discreet glance at Eliza. The woman got up and paced the room for some time before she began talking.

"I knew these young men, both of them. I heard they were captured by the Nazis and taken to a German concentration camp. We were in the same battalion when the German soldiers surrounded us. Many of our comrades were killed, but some of us managed to escape and hide in the woods. We had only a tiny hope for survival. Your sons risked their own lives by helping me to stay alive. I feel with all my loving heart—they are alive and will come back to you."

Eliza wept.

"You don't have to believe me. I don't want to hurt you by giving you false hopes, but I saw your sons with my own eyes, and I owe them my life and the life of my son...."

The woman hesitated for a moment, as if she wanted to add something else—something very important—but seeing the distress she had already caused, rose to leave. A sudden pain seized her whole body. She was obviously exhausted, physically and emotionally. Eliza took her to Rebecca's room. She reminded her so much of her own daughter.

Eliza and Samuel talked about the fate of their sons until late at night. Now they had hopes that Mark and Leon would come back home soon, but their hopes started to dwindle after hearing such horrific news from this unknown and mysterious woman.

* * * * *

In the morning, a freezing rain had frosted the roads with sleet and ice, before giving way to mountains of snow, white and sparkling. A swirling wind tossed it into the air, gusting, playing with snowflakes and throwing them onto windows, plastered with winter frost. The snowfall didn't stop during the night, covering the whole town with the white powder.

The woman appeared in the kitchen with her child. She wore Rebecca's red dress, and if not for her glossy, raven hair and brown eyes, she could easily have been taken for Rebecca. Though she looked a little rested, Eliza saw the dark circles under her eyes. Her child grasped the woman's hand, as if afraid of losing his mother, and looked around him at the unfamiliar environment. While Eliza busied herself preparing breakfast, the woman helped her wash the dishes and clean the kitchen.

An old Russian samovar was puffing in the middle of the table. Eliza ladled out porridge with hot milk onto every plate. They ate in silence, paying attention only to the boy, who hurriedly swallowed the delicious food, licking his spoon clean. He was a very cute, well-mannered and quiet little wonder, who had managed to survive such incredible conditions of cold and hunger.

As they drank their tea, the woman broke the silence, "I need to talk to both of you. It's very important, but I feel too weak now. I have to find the right words to describe to you the story of my survival. I want to tell you who I am and how much I have suffered, how I was betrayed by the old man with whom I stayed while waiting for Mark and Leon to return for me. I had to leave his house and to wander around in the woods for a long time until an old woman helped me to bring my child to life...." She closed her eyes and stopped talking.

Watching the young woman, Eliza realized that their guest had probably merely slept last night. After breakfast, the woman went upstairs and appeared again only in the afternoon. The boy was still asleep.

They had been waiting for her to have their afternoon tea. A pale candle burned in the middle of the table, throwing whimsical shadows on the white tablecloth. Just as they sat peacefully around the table, and the woman was about to tell her story, someone hammered on the door with a fist, loudly and alarmingly. Foreseeing the inevitable, they stopped talking and snuffed out the candle. The silence lasted for some minutes before the beating on the door started again but now louder and more impatiently.

Finally, Samuel had to get up and unlock the door. A gust of cold wind snapped it out of his hands and threw a heap of heavy snow into the house. Two men dressed in winter coats and dark fur hats, burst into the house from the bliz-zard. It was the secret police, the KGB. An ominous quiet fell heavily over the room. They all knew what this sudden appearance meant. The men stood at the threshold for a while, looking around the room with brash, inquisitive eyes.

The brutal words of the men, addressed to the young wo-man, rushed into the house along with the cold air.

"Who are you? How did you get here? Where are your documents?"

And with undue familiarity, they approached her.

"We have a warrant for your arrest."

They forced the woman to get up and grabbed her by the arm.

"Answer our questions."

"I don't have any documents," she admitted. Her face suddenly became white as snow. A clammy cold sweat covered her upper lip.

"Very well then, hurry up. You'll go with us." The man stared at her, struggling to control his annoyance.

Whereupon, she got up without any hesitation or fear and glared at the two men who were waiting for her at the doorway.

"I am a soldier, you are making a mistake."

Then, she turned to Eliza. "I'm sure that this is a serious mistake, and I'll be back."

She kissed her crying child, whom Eliza had brought from the bedroom, then warmly embraced Eliza and Samuel and whispered into Eliza's ear, "Please take care of Alexander, my son until I return. Take care of him, as if he were your own grandchild."

Tears streamed down her cheeks as she embraced her son for the last time. Eliza threw her warm Orenburg shawl around the woman's shoulders, and the two men pushed her roughly to the door. Finally, the woman turned to Eliza:

"If your sons ever come back, tell them that I am alive....My name is Rita" She hadn't finished her sentence when one of the men struck her across the face.

"Shut up, bitch!" You'll talk to us at the office. And now move, move fast. Your time is up."

And with those words they disappeared into the night. No one ever saw or heard from her again. No one ever knew who she was or where she had come from.

When the door slammed behind the woman, Eliza ran after her, but they had vanished into the white mist of the heavily falling snow....

* * * * *

"What about the child?" Eduardo asked impatiently.

During those hours, he had followed Alex's story carefully, trying to put the different parts together, to find the way to his own fate. Alex paused to take a sip of coffee and asked the waiter to bring him another cup. Eduardo was desperate to hear the rest of the story and waited impatiently for Alex to empty his last cup.

"Well, you can imagine what a storm her fate created in the hearts of Eliza and Samuel. Sometimes, the destiny of a stranger can touch you more deeply than your own fate. The life of this innocent woman was taken away before their very eyes. They could not forget that scene as long as they lived. Strangely enough, after the woman had been taken away, Eliza found in a pocket of the woman's coat a photograph of her in a delicate oval frame. In this photo, she was wearing an elegant dress, and a cascade of luxuriant raven-black hair beautifully set off her modeled profile and her sad, wistful gaze. The frame was made of gold and skillfully decorated with small stones. Eliza stowed this picture away for it was the only reminder they had of that tragic night. The child, Alex, stayed with them. They loved him deeply and cared for him, as if he were their own grandson."

"Did Mark and Leon come back from that awful war?"

"Be patient, Eduardo. They waited for their sons to come back. In their small town everybody was greeting their children who had returned from the war, everyone, except for them. During that time, Eliza and Samuel aged tremendously. It would have been an even more difficult time for them if they had not had the obligation to care for this boy, who brought solace to their grieving hearts."

Eduardo interrupted Alex, "Alex, please tell me first what happened afterwards. What do you know about that woman? Did they ever find her? So, maybe both of their sons were alive after all? Maybe the woman was telling the truth? I am beginning to suspect that both brothers were alive—but my story will come later. I want to hear the end of your narrative first. Please go on."

Alex sat for a while as if trying to remember something and then took an old watch out his pocket and looked at it. It was time to go to the train station to meet Eleanor.

"Look, Eduardo, I really have to go now to meet my wife.

I will have to postpone my story until later tonight. Would you like to join me? I can only imagine the startled expression on my wife's face when she sees us together."

He got up at almost the same time as Eduardo who looked quite disappointed.

"No, thank you. I would rather meet you at the exhibittion. I need to take a walk and digest your story. I am beginning to sense a connection. So, see you soon," Eduardo said as he pulled on his jacket.

Chapter Twenty-One
Eleanor's Discovery

$\mathcal{E}$leanor woke up from a strange dream. She was on a train, heading toward an unknown destination. It looped along the naked, barren and dismal plateaus, blanketed with the first frost of the season. Could it be just the memory of her last conversation with Leon before he died? He often spoke to her about the war, the woman he loved and lost, about his hopes and dreams, and the courage he needed to fight for them. With his death, she lost her closest friend, her confidante. He was a great man. Alex was different from his father, perhaps softer, not a fighter at all, trading his soul for fame. Oh, how much she hated having to go to New York for the opening of yet another of Alex's exhibitions! After Leon's death, they began drifting farther apart day by day. Why did Alex never want to admit it to her, pretending to be blind? She was longing to walk away from their marriage, to scream, to be free from the chains of his love, but recently he had become so loving again. He was totally lost after his father's sudden death. She still loved some of Alex' quailties: his tenderness, his ability to listen and communicate with people. She appreciated his knowledge, his zest for life, his charm. However, she realized lately that she was wed not only to him but to the whole package of his selfish persona-lity, his constant striving for fame, his numerous affairs with other women, along with her own loneliness and unhappyness.

Still, she remembered how deeply she had fallen in love with Alex, but it was so long ago....

* * * * *

Alex's life was full of events. A famous artist, he possessed perspicacious wit, incredible strength and energy that imbued all the space around him.

He generally spoke with enthusiasm. His speech was exciting, captivating, and he always remembered to invite the other person to participate in the conversation by asking many questions. He usually avoided long monologues, especially the ones in which he elaborated at great length. Notwithstanding, when he spoke he dominated the room. It was impossible not to listen to him, not to look at him, as well as not to fall under the spell of his charm. He knew more than anyone else and recalled almost everything he had read or heard. He possessed an unusual memory, besides being enamored of poetry and music, to which he devoted most of his time. To crown it all, he had the spiritual beauty of a powerful personality and at the same time unpredictable cruelty. He stood out from the crowd by versatility of knowledge and profound erudition, but under the circumstances he had enough humility to remain in the background. And for all of these qualities, he was loved by his friends and students.

He was called the "Renaissance man" and was the favorite professor, and the most popular teacher in the academy. His lectures were always a one-man-show that drew more than 500 students to his every performance. His subject was the history of Flemish and Dutch art of the seventeenth century. In addition to his profound knowledge of art, Professor Alexander Gold was a handsome man with a deep baritone voice and seductive manners. Of course, all the girls were in love with him. The rumors had been circulating that he had never been married but had numerous love affairs. As for Eleanor, she too was fascinated by him and, like many others before her, came under his spell.

* * * * *

There would come a time, she worried, when her behavior would unpredictably diverge from the wisdom with which she always conducted her life. She accepted it as inevitability and followed her desires without any realization of their fatal consequences. Obsessive love of a man had never happened to her the way she had imagined it. She denied her feelings, knowing in her heart that she had not yet met the man to whom she would give her heart without any regrets. She had learned one important thing in life—first to think, then to act in order to avoid any major mistakes. It was hard to follow this line because her emotions yielded to desire, to irrationality, even though her mind told her to act differently. For a long time, she buffeted with her intense longing for love. Eleanor lived in her own world of disillusion until she had encountered an eerie feeling that she mistakenly took for real love. How could she have known that her passion for art would generate love for a man who represented her ideal image of an artist?

Flemish art and the life of Anthony Van Dyck became her obsession. Nevertheless, she couldn't persuade herself that it was only Van Dyck who influenced her thoughts. Like other girls in her class, she wanted Dr. Gold to notice her, not realizing that from the very beginning he was drawn to his beautiful student with the attentive eyes and rapt attention.

Eleanor was mesmerized not only by his knowledge but by how passionately he delivered his lectures. The passion of his teaching was transmuted for the students into a profound appreciation of art. She began to spend hours in various libraries, reading books on Anthony Van Dyck. Eleanor became familiar with the work of the most famous scholars on Flemish art, including the Belgian art historian Max Roozes, the German—Wilhelm Bode, the English expert Lionel Cust, and the Russian—Andrei Somov. She began to put her thoughts on paper.

The day before her appointment with Alex Gold, it was almost midnight when she finished working. In spite of fatigue, she was only half asleep when she finally turned off her computer, repeating in her mind again and again what she would have to tell Professor Gold about her discovery. Slowly, she sank into dreamful slumber.

* * * * *

In her fitful sleep, she was haunted by blurry images of Anthony Van Dyck himself, who had the face of Alexander Gold. She saw his sitters: King Charles I, Henrietta-Maria, his wife and numerous ladies-in-waiting with whom Van Dyck supposedly had love affairs. All those portraits stood against the wall in her bedroom. One by one, they were coming to life. Charles I proudly galloped on a horse around her bedroom. Henrietta-Maria and Margaret Lemon—Van Dyck's temperamental mistress, Lady Venetia Kenelm, whom he painted on her death bed, and many others noisily discussed the latest events in England, while Van Dyck was deeply engaged in painting a new portrait. To Eleanor's surprise, it was her portrait, and it was Professor Gold, not Van Dyck, who was executing it.

She looked around, the noisy crowd suddenly disappeared, and she found herself in an oval-shaped studio with heavy red draperies. It was chaotically piled with works of art, books and sculptures. The evening dusk totally mantled the room, and only whimsical shadows of its previous guests still remained on the walls. She sat on the edge of a sofa, her hands crossed on her knees. She seemed to be crestfallen as she stared helplessly at the face of the painter. Her look pierced through the invisible wall of space, directly at him, straight into his eyes, shivering with the evening cold. The painter too stared at her for some time, smiling only with the corners of his lips, and then left the room. He soon came back with a blanket and wrapped it around her body. His touch brought to life a consuming desire that was cruel, vivid and frightening. She realized her fear was real when he put his arms around her. Under the shimmering moonlight, rippling through the white curtains, she watched his face seized by emotions. She felt his hot breath on her skin as they plunged into a powerful flux of passion. In her sleep, they were both overwhelmed, happy, exhausted....

* * * * *

Eleanor woke up late with a splitting headache. Her night dream remained vivid and tangible. She still felt his touch on her skin, and her fear reflected in the penetrating green eyes of Alexander Gold. Eleanor took a cold shower and immediately went back to the computer. She wished that her father, whom she had lost only two months ago, could have been alive to share with him her troubled thoughts, but she was all alone in the world.

Eleanor had neither close friends nor relatives. So, she consoled herself with books, mostly art books, poetry, novels and biographies. Her days went by with increasing melancholy and loneliness. She grew aloof from her fellow students, while plunging deeper inward and withdrawing even more into her shell.

She took refuge in studies, and her obsession with the work of Van Dyck helped her to overcome her hours of confinement and solitude. Eleanor had never been daunted by the difficulties in the way—life had taught her how to be a fighter. And yet she was too passive in her personal life. All her schoolmates were dating—except for her. She hadn't yet given a thought to her feelings for Dr. Gold, but one thing she knew for sure—she was scared of him and of his profound knowledge of art and literature, but most of all she was scared by her own physical attraction to him.

* * * * *

This morning, however, Eleanor's mood was lightened by the forthcoming meeting with Professor Alexander Gold.

Although it was already deep fall, Indian summer was still holding on to the sky, unwilling to leave and to yield to the demand of the coming fall. The sky hovered low, like an open falling parachute. Eleanor nervously walked a couple of times around the building. She still had about ten minutes before her appointment. Finally, she pushed the elevator button to the third floor and found herself in a beautiful foyer, almost round in shape, with soft, dark red draperies on both sides of a big window, overlooking the city in a misty, humid cloud. The young and attractive secretary acknowledged Eleanor with a well-trained grimace and ushered her to the professor's office.

Professor Gold had a magnificent office with a view on the center city. Quaint, cherry-wood articles of furniture, Old Masters paintings, antiques and artifacts exuded sophistication and good taste. All of these contributed to the dignified atmosphere of the room. On a small table near the window he kept all his regalia, awards and souvenirs, brought from his numerous trips. Two small bookshelves were filled with recent art journals. The walls were also adorned with some unusual watercolors and pencil drawings by famous contemporary American artists. Eleanor was mesmerized by a masterly executed drawing, hanging above his desk. The painting depicted a totally naked woman with long dark hair, writhing in pain. She realized that the portrait was painted by Professor Gold himself. Who was this mysterious woman? Eleanor averted her gaze, deeply disturbed by the drawing.

"Sit down, please. What can I do for you? Is it still hot outside? Who would ever think that the beginning of October could be so hot?" he said reluctantly.

His face was genial, but his voice revealed certain hostility. Could it be her imagination because she was too nervous and too tense, or perhaps she expected a different kind of greeting? How she could have ever guessed that this was simply his tactic for attracting this naïve girl by feigning his total indifference? He didn't wait for her answer and moved right away to the main question.

"Did you come to see me as an art historian, an expert on Van Dyck, or do you have some difficulties in following my course?"

Only now, did she notice that he was watching her with some attention, and the expression of indifference on his face was replaced by a look of bewilderment. He leaned forward, as if he wanted to see her better. His keen, expressive eyes bored into her with some hidden curiosity.

Eleanor was about to cry. She didn't expect to be greeted with such coldness. After all, she made a discovery. She needed to tell him about two portraits attributed to Van Dyck but supposedly painted by his teacher, Rubens. They were the portraits of Isabella Brant, the first wife of Rubens, who died young of tuberculosis, leaving him with three children, and the portrait of Susanna Faurment, a sister of Rubens' second wife, Helena, whom he married when she was only fifteen and he was fifty-three. According to some sources, Rubens had a secret love affair with Susanna Faurment.

"I followed your lectures very carefully, professor, and I have to agree with you—it is amazing that every painting has its own mysterious destiny and its own history as well as the artist himself, and of course his sitters," she began talking, trying to capture his attention.

"It's very exciting to search for the history of paintings and the fate of their artists, and finally…to discover step by step how it is all connected," she continued, throwing at him a stealthy glance.

He looked inquisitively into her face and agreed readily with her statement, watching how she slowly put all her paperwork in front of him and spread it all over his desk. After a minute of total concentration, she began to present arguments about her discovery, weighing her words very carefully while her heart throbbed and her cheeks flushed.

He was impressed but tried to hide his intense interest, looking over the copies of the documents. A copy of a letter by someone named James A. Schmidt caught his attention. The letter was in Russian and published in the old Russian magazine called Старые Годы (Old Times).

"Do you read Russian?" The professor seemed surprised.

"Yes, just a little bit. My father spoke some Russian, but I heard that you are fluent in Russian. I thought you could probably help me to fully understand the content of this letter."

"Yes, in fact I can. The author claimed that the Rubens' signature was on the reverse sides of the original frames on both paintings you have just mentioned. Why didn't you ask your father to help you?"

"He was very ill and died two months ago."

"I am sorry to hear it, Eleanor."

It was the first time that he had called her by name. His eyes warmed and from cold blue turned into soft green. It struck her before that his eyes were blue, tending to grey or green.

"Had you been close to your father?"

"Yes, he was my best friend. I would rather not talk about it."

He gave a nod of understanding and switched the subject back to Van Dyck's portraits.

"So, I summarize your statement. According to Wilhelm Bode, both those paintings were painted by Rubens. They were bought from the collection of Count Choiseul of France by Catherine the Great with the attribution to Rubens. Is that so?"

"Yes, but after the collection was bought by Andrew Mellon from the Soviet authorities and removed from the Hermitage Museum, and finally placed in the National Gallery of Art in Washington, both portraits were attributed to Van Dyck."

Reviewing her paperwork, Professor Gold concluded suddenly, "Well, you did a great piece of research. You should go to Washington to meet the National Gallery curator of Dutch and Flemish art and see what he says about your discovery." His voice was now much friendlier, though she didn't see any trace of excitement in his eyes. He thought for a minute and then added.

"Actually, I may join you. I would love to see his reaction when he learns about your research."

Eleanor was numbed—he didn't even glance at her, as if it had been already decided between them that they were going to Washington. The professor called his secretary on the phone,

"Suzie, dear, can you find out when is the next time I am free from lecturing. Next Wednesday? Fine, thank you. Please make an appointment for me on that day with the curator of Flemish Art at the National Gallery of Art in Washington and one night in my favorite hotel. Great! Thank you, my friend."

He turned to Eleanor and looked her over with some pleasure. Their eyes locked. "So, next Wednesday, Eleanor, I'll meet you at the train station around ten in the morning. Prepare all your paperwork. Agreed?"

She blushed and nodded disarmingly, casting a shy look at him. How could she object if the matter had already been settled regardless of whether she had agreed or not? Her thoughts were in disarray. Was it true that she was going with Professor Gold himself to the National Gallery of Art to present her discovery to the famous gallery curator?

"By the way," he interrupted her train of thought, "we'll be returning the next day. I'll make some plans for us in the evening. Don't worry about the hotel. I'll take care of it."

Seeing Eleanor's bewilderment, he smiled and approached her. Bending over the chair next to her face, he spoke softly, "You are an exceptional girl, Eleanor, and I'm sure you'll enjoy our trip."

He reached for her hand and gently squeezed it. She sensed the warmth and strong energy emanating from his body. In a hurry, Eleanor collected all her paperwork and put it in a folder.

"Thank you, professor, for listening to me and taking me seriously."

"Alex, you can call me Alex. And you are very welcome indeed, Eleanor. So, don't forget, Wednesday, at ten."

He went back to his desk, a clear demonstration that the audience was over.

Walking back from his office, she felt giddy and confused. His pretty secretary stared at her with an oblique smile at the corners of her painted lips.

"Goodbye, dear, I'll make all the arrangements for Wednesday.... Have a nice trip."

Eleanor didn't reply and hastily opened the door to the staircase instead of taking the elevator. Later, it crossed her mind that she hadn't asked him to get a separate room for her, but it was already too late to return to his office with such a foolish question. She brushed off this sudden unsettling thought, hoping this ticklish matter would eventually settle itself.

She turned once again in her mind everything she had heard before about the professor from her close friend, Stella.

Stella, who had known about the forthcoming meeting, had forewarned Eleanor: "Remember, Eleanor, people say that if someone just once gets into his aura, they remain there as his prisoner or his servant for the rest of their lives. He does not like to talk much about himself, but he is always eager to listen, leaning toward the speaker and fixing his sharp, penetrating eyes on the person. The color of his eyes usually changes according to his moods, events or circumstances. If a person he speaks with interests him, his eyes change into a soft, warm-green color, if indifferent—they turn icy blue. When he is angry, they are cold and transparently grey."

"How do you know such details?" Eleanor was flabbergasted.

Stella blushed and turned away from Eleanor's intense gaze.

"Have you been involved with him?"

"Eleanor, everybody—but you—knows he is a womanizer. I was in love with him once. We had a brief love affair some time ago. It's all over now. Why are you asking? Are you his next victim?" She laughed.

"Please, stop, Stella. I am not his victim and will never be. Maybe I have chosen him as my victim. We will see."

"Don't try to fool me, Eleanor. You are also obsessed with our charming Professor Gold. Aren't you?"

* * * * *

"What is the next stop? Do you know?"

Eleanor heard a whiny voice, which barely reached her consciousness as she tried to shake off nagging memories. She cast a sidelong glance at a middle-aged man, sitting across from her on the opposite bench of the moving train. She looked him over carefully, thinking that by his polished looks, big belly and well-nourished face he could be a politician. Eleanor didn't feel like getting involved in any conversation.

"I am not sure. I am afraid I dozed off for some time."

"I was watching you. What was your dream about?" The man's eyes darted lustfully about Eleanor's face, appraising her beauty.

Eleanor turned to the window, ignoring his question and watching the running platform of the train station. At the same time, the conductor announced that they were arriving in New York. There was the usual movement among the passengers, collecting their luggage and forming a long line to the exit. Eleanor was not in a hurry. She slowly buttoned her coat and put on lipstick.

The man continued staring at her with the same lustful

look. "Is anybody meeting you at the station? I could offer you a dinner in a nice restaurant." His well-groomed face expressed self-satisfaction.

Eleanor shook her head, hardly restraining her fret. "I am honored by your offer, sir, but unfortunately I have a previous engagement."

She saw a look of disappointment cross his round, double-chinned face. And then, after some moments, she added, glaring at him in defiance, "To be honest, I would not accept your offer anyway. You are too polished, too well-organized. I don't like people like that, but thank you anyway...."

She picked up her light suitcase and moved closer to the exit. Her bad mood deepened as she started thinking about her husband's new exhibition, the adoring crowd, the flattering remarks and the pretentious smiles that awaited her at the museum. The two-hour trip had given her a splitting headache, and now all she wanted was a hot shower and a nap.

* * * * *

A short while later, Alex walked to the train station alone. A small crowd was waiting on the platform for the incoming train. As soon as the train pulled into the station, finally losing its speed, Alex saw his wife. She got off the train, resplendent like a movie star with her long, curly, chestnut hair. Elegantly dressed in a long white coat and white boots with high heels, without any make-up except for a slight touch of pink lipstick, she had never looked more glorious. Smiling happily, Alex embraced her and kissed her on both cheeks, greeting her effusively.

"You look gorgeous, Eleanor. I missed you, darling, and I have so much to tell you."

"Not now, Alex, please. I am too tired," she replied in a flat, indifferent voice, getting into a cab.

"You didn't tell me where you are going." The cab driver turned his head, staring at Eleanor.

"Please, take me to the Hotel Meridian," Eleanor answered plainly, and looking at Alex, she tried to justify her intentions, "I need to freshen up a bit, but you continue your trip. I'll meet you at the gallery shortly perhaps. Otherwise, call me after the show. I'll join you for dinner."

Eleanor smiled, but Alex sensed tension in her voice. He was visibly upset that Eleanor hadn't expressed any interest in attending the opening of his new exhibition.

Chapter Twenty-Two
Confrontation

𝓔leanor climbed under the covers and pulled the blanket over her head. She managed to snatch an hour's nap, but instead of feeling refreshed afterwards, she felt tense and nervous. She rose and, putting on her warm robe, looked out the window. High above, thunderheads were gathering and, forming a fast-streaming river, undulating in the sky. This scene evoked her memories of another day in her life, the day of the confrontation with Alex, the day that remained in her thoughts these past years. "A dull rainy day began with splashes of rain and wind...."

* * * * *

A dull rainy day began with melodic splashes of rain and wind. Eleanor remained by the window, watching the first drops of rain reach the pavement. She stood there for quite a long time until she noticed the rain had begun to let up, and the wind was emitting a loud moan, waltzing with the flickering leaves. The wind vacillated for some time and then slowly deflated, like a balloon, puffing out cold air along the empty street.

She was waiting for Alex to pick her up, but he was late as usual. He had a habit of making people wait for him. In a way, she was glad he was late—he had given her more time to think about him, their relationship and their future together. Finally, her worries of the last two days were replaced by clear thinking.

Her thoughts were interrupted by a loud knock on the door, announcing Alex's arrival. Alex, who never used the doorbell, but instead, banged on the door impatiently and annoyingly. When she opened the door, he strode confidently into the room, bringing with him the effervescence of his loud and cheerful personality that filled the room. A crisp burst of air entered the room, modulating the warm temperature.

"You brought with you the smell of wind and the taste of leaves," Eleanor whispered, taking from his hands a huge bouquet of yellow and red poplar leaves and inhaling their freshness.

"They are the color of your hair," he said, approaching her and touching her wavy tresses.

She moved swiftly from him, laughing. "Don't rumple my hair please."

But he didn't listen to her—he thought she had probably forgotten that today was their anniversary—exactly one year since their first trip to Washington. Just two weeks ago, he had proposed, and she had almost accepted, but today, to his surprise, the diamond engagement ring was not on her finger.

"Oh, I almost forgot," he smiled mischievously and put a small box on the table. "Open it. It's my present for you. I want to give you something memorable, Eleanor. I missed you that whole bloody week when you suddenly disappeared from my life. But please, darling, remember that there's not another woman in the world that could make me happy—there's only you."

He opened the small box, containing a hand-painted brooch. On a small, lacquered oval, Alex had painted Eleanor's face. It was a masterpiece, made in the unique style of old Russian miniature portraits.

Eleanor put her arms around him. "Oh, Alex, you could not have given me a lovelier present. You know how much I value your work, and how grateful I am for your understanding. I truly appreciate it. But I didn't forget our anniversary, darling. I have a present for you too."

She went to her bedroom and brought back a package, wrapped in red paper. "What is it? I thought you had forgotten...."

"Open it."

She helped him unwrap her present. It was a painting Eleanor had done for him. Alex noted that it was very well executed, but extremely odd. The painting depicted a late autumn day enveloped in a dense fog with a long road in an old park. Three silhouettes—two men and a woman, holding hands – were walking down the road. Their images were almost invisible. There was something very peaceful and yet disturbing in their lonely figures among tall naked trees and heavy clouds brooding low above them, as if ready to fall to earth. Looking at this painting, Alex could not suppress a feeling of unease, as if he could sense in it a premonition of a gathering thunderstorm.

He put his arms around her. "What inspired you to paint this beautiful picture, Eleanor?"

"I don't know, Alex, I can't explain it. It is like a dream that I wanted to make real. Please, don't ask me to explain. And please, darling, don't press me any further about our marriage. I will let you know when I am ready."

He noticed that she spoke with certain sadness in her voice. He thought that any other woman would jump at the opportunity to become the wife of such a famous artist, but not Eleanor. She still remained a woman of mystery and puzzled him by her silent resistance, which made her even more desirable to him.

They walked outside into a deserted street, chilly and mute. The first dim streetlights were coming on and throwing yellow flashes into the air, permeated with heavy drops of rain. But then abruptly, just as it had started, the rain ebbed. Feeble moonlight broke through the layers of clouds.

Eleanor gazed wistfully at Alex, "I like the melancholy of rainy days. Somehow, it reminds me of my childhood." He didn't reply, enjoying the sound of her deep voice.

She hesitated for a moment and then resumed, "Look, Alex, we have known each other for such a long time, and yet you have never told me anything about yourself, your childhood."

"Well, my childhood....Where shall I start? My memories are so scattered, so vague, just small fragments here and there. I guess...I have always tried to block them. I remember my grandmother very well. I mistakenly thought she was my mother. We lived in a small town in Belorussia. Soon after my father returned from the war, we moved to Leningrad...."

"Is that all?" Eleanor was visibly disappointed, "Do you have any memories of your life in Leningrad?"

He floundered for a moment, "No, not much, really. I remember well many rainy days in Leningrad, fused with a deep melancholy, like today, here in Philadelphia. I recall a small room in a communal flat on the fourth floor of an old four-story building, located on Griboedov's Canal, named after the Russian poet, Alexander Griboedov. It was a narrow street, paved with uneven bricks. Our window overlooked a large, empty and desolate wasteland with dying grass, scattered dirty bottles and piles of trash. I was ten or eleven years old and afraid to look out the window on that unknown and mysterious field. Once, I heard from the neighbor that a young sailor had been murdered there, and his corpse had lain unattended for a long time. I often thought about the young sailor and his fate. It left a deep impression on my young soul."

"Can you describe to me a communal flat, Alex?"

"I don't even know how to explain it to you, Eleanor. There was a long corridor with many doors, seventeen or so in our flat. For all of us, there was only one kitchen and one toilet, no bathroom. That's how we lived in those days."

"Why have you never told me about it?"

"Because it's too sad.... Let us not talk about sad things. Perhaps, my father is more inclined to talk about his past because he still lives there— his presence in the present time is only an illusion. He exists just for me in this world which is foreign for him. He knows how much I need and love him, and how desperately lonely I'll be without him. What are you thinking about, Eleanor?"

She touched his hand. "I am thinking about you, Alex. You know that your life matters a great deal to me."

"Oh, God, I have been waiting to hear these words from you for a long time."

"I'm sorry you have never told me about your past, your grandmother and what happened to your real mother. Perhaps it could help me to better understand you."

"I don't like to talk about my past. Too many bad memories, and, as you can guess, I am a happy man now."

"I understand. I am sorry, darling. It's so stupid of me. I'm really sorry."

He put his arms around her, and Eleanor thought maybe she hadn't tried hard enough to understand him better, to become part of his life. Perhaps, climbing the stairs of success, pursuing his career, he just wanted to forget what he had been yesterday. It was impossible to detect any emotion from looking at him, as if he wanted to keep a distance between his remote, unhappy past and his successful present. They walked in silence for the rest of the way.

The colorful autumn leaves were prattling, rustling and dying under their footsteps. The streets were shimmering with wistful autumn hues. The city exhaled the smell of leaves, fused with humidity. The dark sky hovered low over its tall edifices. In the degraded autumn colors, the city looked washed out and almost surreal....

* * * * *

They entered a small, cozy restaurant on the twelfth floor and took a table near the window. The city was scarcely visible through misty sheets of rain. Eleanor glanced at Alex and was struck by the sad expression on his face. But she knew there was one more step to be taken tonight. It had been on her mind for a long time now—to tell him everything that had been bothering her lately. Only he was the first one to start the conversation, sensing some trouble in the air.

"Eleanor, tell me what's on your mind? I want to keep you from making a mistake. I want to marry you. You know that....I thought it had already been tacitly decided between the two of us."

As he spoke, his eyes shone feverishly, and he reminded her of a small, scared rabbit. He poured some sparkling water into her glass, and then he again focused his attention on the engagement ring, still missing from her finger.

"Where is the ring, Eleanor?"

"O, stop worrying, Alex. I took it off this morning to wash dishes and probably forgot to put it back."

He sipped some water from the glass.

"It's all decided between us, isn't it? You belong to me now, Eleanor, and there shouldn't be any secrets between us. I hope —"

He hadn't finished his sentence when she interrupted him dismissively, "I don't belong to anybody, Alex. Remember? Don't try to run my life. We have talked about this before. I am not saying I have lost my feeling for you, but, yes, I have fallen in love with someone else. I didn't plan it to happen. I am telling you the truth. Anyhow, you have nothing to be afraid of. It is probably just an illusion, a figment of my sick imagination."

"I hate it when you talk like this. I don't understand you. Just tell me the truth."

"Are you sure you want to hear what I'm about to say?"

"Let's get into this damn thing and get it over with."

"Alright then, what would you like to know? There's not much to say. It was a brief encounter, nothing more. Are you jealous?"

"Yes, I am. I'm not a prude, but I can't imagine you in the arms of another man. I hope you understand. Let's make it clear once and for all. Yes, I'm jealous, but I can forgive you if there is no emotion involved, only your imagination."

"Alex, I am sorry. Let's forget about it, really. I am deeply sorry."

"You have hurt me, Eleanor, but I love you. I've no choice but to forgive you. Just tell me who is he. Do I know him?"

She smiled "It's you, Alex, your own copy. Look in the mirror."

"Stop joking, Eleanor. With you, I never know what is real and what your artistic imagination is."

She laughed. "Please, stop asking me about a phantom. There is no point in discussing this any further. I repeat— you have nothing to worry about. Actually, you interrupted me when I was talking about my imagination. There is one important subject for me that you so skillfully avoided discussing. Do you know that with you I lost the chastity of my imagination? Do you know that I can't paint anymore—you killed my desire to become an artist?"

"You changed the subject but go on anyway," he demanded.

Alex filled up two crystal glasses with wine. "You like this wine, it's your favorite."

He handed her the glass, but she didn't touch it. He noticed a kind of hostility in her eyes, as if small powerful sparks of fire had burst out of her soul.

"Look, Eleanor, you move in such a dangerous direction. I'm not defending my actions. I'm well aware of my faults. You should try to understand—it was always my ambition to achieve fame and success, just as I dreamed about your

147

future," he snapped, eluding her intense look. Then he added, "I love my life fervently, and from the time I succeeded in becoming an artist, I have lived with the strong goal of reaching the top. I have fallen into the abyss many times, but I have always recovered."

She edged in, "And consumed with artistic greed, you've descended deeper and deeper into the desire to reach for the stars. In your heart, you have failed yourself, but you wanted to be reborn in the work of your students. Is that so, Alex? Is that what you wanted to say?"

"Actually, yes, you are my star, my future. I'm not going to give you up."

She had never heard him speak this way before that very moment. He bent over, trying to overcome his bad temper, and took a gulp from the glass of red wine. Red drops hung from his beard and then dropped back into the glass. She became paralyzed with fear.

He noticed the fear on her face and stopped talking. A long pause, interrupted only by Beethoven's 9th Symphony in the background, gave him time to ponder her words.

"Yes, I decided to guide you through the unintelligible paths to the road of fame and success."

He coughed and gulped down a whole glass of wine at once.

Eleanor took advantage of the moment and continued his thought, adding some sarcasm to her words, "Oh, no. You can argue about it endlessly, but you did not care about my achievements—you only strived for your own fame. Am I right, Alex? Tell me if I am right?" And without waiting for his reply, she went on, "You have known for a long time now that your real talent vanished the moment you became greedy for fame and recognition. At the beginning of your career, your distorted vision of the world seemed amazing. However, you ran out of fresh ideas of your own, and it was only by gathering around you some extraordinary people, you managed to keep some of your past success. Portraits of the rich and famous....You remind me of your idol, Anthony Van Dyck...."

"I'm afraid, Eleanor, you don't really understand my motives for painting portraits. Don't you think our conversation is becoming very intriguing, or should I say...hurtful?"

"I am really sorry, I didn't mean to hurt you, Alex, but you put chains on my mind and my soul. You distorted my sense of clarity, my ability to think independently. You slowly pushed me into the abyss, the darkness of your own ego."

"Hell, no...Eleanor, please stop!"

He raised his hand as if trying to protect himself from her hurtful words. Yet she could not stop. The words kept pouring out of her heart, demanding to liberate her from her own pain. She wanted to inflict the same pain on him, instead of showing him the gratitude that he was longing for. She narrowed her eyes and stared at him.

"Shall I continue?" She ignored his faint gesture of protest as she prepared to build a podium for his final execution. Only then, did she notice Alex's face twisted with pain, his hands pressed together.

He strived to quench the flow of her painful words, but instead, whispered in a broken voice, "You won, Eleanor. Please, don't go on. It hurts too much. You managed to discover the truth behind my façade of wellbeing which I tried to hide even from you. But...."

He was speaking now to himself, almost forgetting her presence, "But you still don't know me. Anyhow, I have my doubts now that you ever loved me, Eleanor." He finally smiled rather childishly and disarmingly.

"Yes, I did love you, and I do now." She stared at him for some time, searching for the right words. "I still love you, Alex. Otherwise, I would not be with you today."

"I trust your words, Eleanor, but you know I want more."

She put her hand on his and said nothing for some time.

Then he spoke again, "You always complicate everything. My life without you would be meaningless. I can try to change for you."

She liked the way he said it. He suddenly looked like a defenseless child.

"I love you the way you are. I don't want you to be different, Alex. I'll be your wife."

"This is the happiest day in my life, Eleanor. In fact, you have made two men happy today at the same time—my father and me." Alex' eyes shone with excitement.

The cold, grey color of his eyes changed into warm green. He closed his arms around her as they stood to leave, but she freed her-self from his embrace.

"It's getting late."

"I'll walk you home. I need to clear my mind anyway after such a turbulent evening. I want to see the ring on your finger again, Eleanor."

"You will."

She smiled at him, thinking that somehow she had managed to stir up Alex's thoughts, put them in disarray. She did want to cause some disturbance in his life, to make him suffer and return to his real self, when he was young and so unbelievably talented, away from his success in painting soulless portraits. Still, she knew that it was not in her power to return him to his past. Now, she began to feel guilty, thinking about his childhood and his lonely life with his father. She really wanted to make him happy and to ease the life of his father, whom she so deeply respected. She tried to suppress a sense of sadness, realizing again that her fate and Alex's had just been sealed forever.

Chapter Twenty-Three
The Exhibition

*A*fter taking Eleanor to the hotel, Alex went straight to the museum. He was deeply hurt by Eleanor's indifference to his work. At the beginning of their marriage, she used to help him finish his portraits with her magical touches, but soon she began losing interest in helping him to create his soulless portraits. After her graduation, she found a job in one of the galleries as a restorer and threw herself passionately into her new duties. She recently lost all curiosity for Alex's work. Alex thought that if his father had been alive, he would have appreciated his success as a portrait painter. He brushed off these disturbing thoughts and tried to concentrate on the events of the day.

When finally Alex entered the exhibit hall, there was only a half hour left before its opening. Eduardo was already there, greeting him with his disarming smile.

"I have been waiting for you for quite some time, Alex. Please hurry up. We still have about thirty minutes left. I want you to be my guide."

Eduardo suddenly stopped, his eyes wide in astonishment as he gazed at a sizable poster with the portrait of a strikingly beautiful woman, painted with strong, slanted brush-strokes. Alex's name, printed in red, stood out above the portrait.

"Whose portrait is this, Alex?"

Eduardo seemed to be somewhat perturbed.

"It's a portrait of my wife. Do you like it?"

"Yes, in fact I think it's a masterpiece."

"It will be the jewel of the exhibition. You will see. My only concern is that no matter how hard I tried to depict Eleanor the way I saw her, the portrait still looked different from the image I was trying to create. Let's not waste our time. I have many more masterpieces to show you." Alex glanced at Eduardo, inviting him to continue their tour.

"I want you to see my early work....Just follow me."

Eduardo noticed that Alex said the last words with pride, which increased his curiosity about Alex's art.

When they stopped in front of a small watercolor in a simple wooden frame, Eduardo was mesmerized by its beauty. It depicted a forest, pinked by the sun, rising above the horizon. The light was almost surreal, as if coming from another world. Its rays slightly touched the earth and the tops of the trees. It conveyed such a subtle feeling, subdued emotion, a magical aura that immediately drew Eduardo into a world of awakening happiness. All his watercolors represented a brilliant display of different colors and impressive new techniques. A wondrous combination of subdued red, bright yellow, deep green and blue impressed Eduardo the most. It was music of colors, recreated from Scriabin's symphony. Altogether, Alex' paintings gave the impression of a mystery behind the melodies of light and color, behind the world of unreality and mystery. Eduardo saw in Alex's watercolors the craftsmanship, combined with an energy and spirit of hope, in addition to a haunting mystical quality.

There were about twenty such watercolors, bursting with the sheer beauty of color and music. Eduardo couldn't take his eyes from Alex's early work. The mastery he achieved in his paintings convinced Eduardo beyond any doubt—Alex was a real genius, almost a magician, who at this point had lost his brush, his sense of color and had finally diverted his energy into art that was unworthy of his talent. He belonged to a different world, the one that he had left for fame and success.

Eduardo's first impression of these masterpieces was that they were extremely powerful. However, he needed time to himself to ruminate over the paintings he had just seen and to see more of Alex's work. The rest of the day, Eduardo went through the hall alone, leaving Alex to enjoy his predictable success.

The remaining paintings were mostly portraits, well executed, but dull. Only one portrait attracted his attention, another portrait of Alex's wife, painted long time ago. Eduardo fixed his eyes on her face. The oblong, pensive eyes with golden glitters held a deep secret. The subdued light with some sudden dark passages intensified the expression of sadness on her spiritual face. Her hands were on the armrests of the chair, and Eduardo had the impression that she was about to get up and leave the room, to fade slowly from the picture into her own secret world of dreams. Somehow, this portrait aroused a tangled recollection of another portrait he had tried to paint almost twenty years ago....This reminiscence brought back some painful moments from his past... the blizzard in New York....

Eduardo's first impulse was to leave immediately, to go back to Italy, but he could not do it. He wanted to hear the story of Alex's parents to the end. He was now more than ever sure that they were related.

Finally, when the crowd thinned, Alex found Eduardo standing before the portrait of Eleanor and pulled him out of the exhibition hall to the street.

"Aren't you going for the reception?" Eduardo wondered.

"No, I don't think so. These last days have been too emotional."

"Your organizers will be disappointed."

"I know, but right now all my energy is directed to solving our puzzle. You probably feel the same way. Don't you?"

Alex and Eduardo stepped outside the museum into the dark that had suddenly fallen over the city. Only the hardly detectable music of the rain, dropping into puddles, disturbed the tranquility of the evening. The autumn air was windless and solemn. The merely visible moonlight tried to rend the clouds. It emitted an eerie glow through their heavy density. Skyscrapers began slowly melting away in the impending twilight, but their merely visible silhouettes still loomed on the dark canvas of the sky. The rain soon stopped. However, it was still humid and rather warm.

"Was your father also an artist?" Alex asked Eduardo, breaking their silence first.

"Actually, yes, but we will talk about my father later. Instead, let's talk about your work. It's your day, Alex. I do want to congratulate you. Your exhibition was a thumping success! You are really a good artist, the way you execute all those portraits—such a marvelous technique. However, I am more impressed by your early work, your love of flamboyant and yet subdued colors. Nevertheless, I noticed a sort of coldness in your late portraits, not the coldness of your sitters, but your indifference to the people whose portraits you paint. Why?"

"May I ask you a simple question, Eduardo? Do you consider yourself a happy man?"

And without waiting for an answer, Alex went on, as if someone had pushed a painful button that he was always afraid to touch. "I always thought that I was a 'relatively' happy man. Why relatively you may ask? Well, to tell you the truth....I am not. In other words, sometimes I just pretend to be happy because I have everything that one's heart could desire—a wife I love, my work, money, success. In spite of all my efforts to live in peace with myself, one thing is missing—I am not in peace with my soul. You see, I am a very emotional person. My work used to be based on my emotions. When painting, I was exhausting my soul, emptying it, and yet I did not feel happy."

"Oh, how well I understand your feelings. Nevertheless, you found a way to escape your overwhelming emotions by creating works of art that didn't need your spiritual input. All it needed were just your skills and your techniques. However, if you take away from me all my desires, all my hopes, all my emotions, I would become a dead man," Eduardo said quietly.

"Well, I appreciate your understanding. Honestly, you can't imagine how often I have unexplained twinges of conscience, but I can't change anything now. I am the one who sold his soul to the devil. Too late…too late now…."

"It is never too late, Alex, to start all over again. I think that I am just beginning to live. Our strange encounter has changed our lives forever, and I am grateful to you for that."

They entered a small, cozy restaurant, where Alex had made a reservation. They sat in its remote corner. Then Eduardo continued, "You know, Alex, I have found in you a kindred spirit, more than a friend, a brother."

Alex raised his eyebrows, "I appreciate your sincerity, Eduardo. I do feel the same way. I am glad we met."

Meanwhile, Eduardo was becoming impatient, eager to learn the fate of the child and the both brothers. It was now obvious to him that Alex could be his cousin, but he was completely unprepared for what he heard next. "Alex, please go on with your story. I am eager to learn what happened."

Alex was finishing his soup. Suddenly, he felt hungry after such a long day at the show. Eduardo patiently waited until Alex pushed away the empty bowl and, delving into the past, began his narration. "Well, this is the most difficult part of the story. This story I also heard from my father….Numb with cold, disoriented and frustrated, wearing wet overcoats, the young soldiers stumbled along the narrow, winding path…."

Chapter Twenty-Four
The Three Soldiers

*N*umb with cold, disoriented and frustrated, wearing wet overcoats, the young soldiers stumbled along the narrow, winding path. The late autumn had eventually come to a standstill. Almost every day now, an incessant morning drizzle stretched into night rainfall. There were only the three of them, rambling blindly through the forest: a slender, young woman with dark, gypsy eyes, dressed in a heavy green uniform with a red cross, and two young soldiers with a striking resemblance to each other. Their bristly, untidy beards looked almost unreal on their youthful faces, covered with a thin coat of mud. They herded together, anxious to find some protection against the wind, the rain and the fog. The trees, wounded by the war, had already shed their leaves and stood almost naked on both sides of the path. Their branches, interlaced above, struggled to resist the northern wind that droned and trumpeted through the devastated rural area. These were the typically cold days of late fall.

Only days before, their small battalion had been surroundded and crushed by a large group of German soldiers. Many of their comrades had been killed, but some managed to escape into the nearby woods. Those who escaped struggled to stay close to each other, making slow headway into the depth of the woods. Shortly afterwards, in a murky fog, they had lost the rest of their friends.

At first, there was no trace of a path leading farther into the wooded area. Soon, they noticed some scattered scrubs, forming a pathway that ran between the tall trees, hardly visible in the distant gloom. They waded through mud until the pathway branched off to the main street of an obscure country village, surrounded by forest. The place was pitch dark and quiet. It met them with a grim and despairing silence. The black night turned the streets into ghostly empty corridors. The houses stood lifeless, their shutters closed.

Mark held Rita's hand in his, trying to give her hope that they would now be able to find a place to rest.

"Don't cry, Rita, we are now in a safe place. Do you see those small dots of light behind the windows? I see them as the lights of hope. We will find a place to stay, darling," he whispered into her ear.

Rita didn't reply. She was fast losing her remaining strength, and her feet would no longer obey her. They were leaden, drowning in the boggy, wet soil. Every step required an incredible effort. Finally, they turned into a side street, moving gingerly and staying close to the houses. They came to a dead end and stopped near a clean, white house with a wicker fence and closed shutters. The house was immersed in the dark night, but some glimmers of light oozed out through small cracks in the shutters. This quiet corner seemed to be only a tiny part of a sleepy, unknown town.

Rita, still holding Mark's hand, pressed her cheek against his wet overcoat. "I am scared, Mark."

In the dark, he saw her lustrous eyes struck by fear. "You should not be afraid, Rita. You are such a brave girl. We are going to be fine."

And then, he turned to Leon. "Look at this house, Leon. Does it remind you of our house?"

He recognized something familiar in this small, neatly painted house with its red brick roof, wisps of gray smoke coming out of the chimney, and snaky ivy twined around the fence. It really did remind them of their own home at the edge of a town, called Nevel. They hesitated, frightened by the muteness of the air, disturbed only by the drops of rain. Not a single shot had been heard in the village, as if the war had rushed past and died away forever.

The front door of the house suddenly opened, and a frightened, stubby old man with a very sinister face, dressed in a dark raincoat, appeared on the doorsteps. A sparse gray beard framed his famished, gaunt face with shrewd, small eyes. Instinctively, they stepped back, startled. The man squinted and scrutinized them incredulously, peering into the dusk of the night. Leon was the first one to take a step forward. At the same time, the old man shone a flashlight on his face.

"Who are you, and what are you doing here?" His voice sounded aggressive.

"We are lost and need a place to stay. We are worn out. Do you know how far away the Nazis are? Tell us please, friend, what's going on around here," Leon said gloomily and came closer to the old man, blinking his eyes from the bright flashlight.

The man's glance rested on Leon's face for a moment, carefully examining him before he replied. "They are in a neighboring town and might be here any time. Meanwhile, don't ask me any questions here—even the night has its eyes and ears. Come in, come in."

He shifted his gaze to Rita and moved aside, letting them enter the house.

They had barely crossed the threshold when the old man swiftly turned the key in the lock. The unexpected guests hovered dubiously near the door, looking around the room and examining the place. The spacious anteroom was cool and dusky, but the rooms were warm. A tiny furnace radiated enough warmth to heat the whole house. A large rustic, oaken table, covered with a clean, white tablecloth, stood in the middle of the room. A small bed in the corner of the room had a colorful quilt. The oil lamp on the bedside-table threw a cone of light on two photographs, hanging on the opposite wall. One of them depicted Vladimir Lenin, standing on the battleship Potemkin while the other one was a portrait of Joseph Stalin, leaning against the red flag.

"We have to apologize for the late intrusion, but we have a young woman among us who needs some help," Mark spoke slowly, supporting Rita, who was about to faint.

The old man began bustling around the room fretfully.

"Why in the world are you standing in the door? Don't tread water. Please come in and sit down, my dear guests. Indeed, all of you should take off your wet overcoats and your dirty boots. And for God sake, leave your dirty duffel-bags at the threshold. Hurry up, hurry up. Meanwhile, I'll boil some water," he demanded in a peremptory tone.

He put some cups, plates and an old samovar on the table and hobbled out of the room, complaining of the early frost and pain in his hips. His loud voice reached them from the hencoop.

"Damnation, it hurts like hell, again. These damn chickens, I have just cleaned the space," he droned on loudly.

While he was outside, getting fresh eggs from his hencoop, and smoked fish from his storage bin, they clustered around the heating furnace.

"I don't like him," Rita said quietly, holding her hands over the heater. Her deathly pale face was covered with red spots.

"Rita, you are running a temperature." Mark put his hand on Rita's forehead.

"I am fine." She pushed Mark's hand away. "I said I do not trust this man."

"Why?" Leon asked, still struggling with his dirty boots.

"He is too nice...perhaps too evasive. What do you think, Mark?"

She turned her attention to Mark, who was mulling pensively over something.

"I don't know what to say. Maybe we are getting too wary of every person around us. We've stopped trusting each other. It's too late to leave this house now anyway. We need some rest and especially you, Rita. And we have not eaten since yesterday."

"Trust my intuition." Rita shook her head emphatically.

They didn't hear when the old man came back and slithered softly through the door, his old polished boots hardly touching the shiny parquet floor. To their great surprise, he held a basket full of eggs, a bunch of smoked fish and a loaf of bread.

"Faugh, damn! It's my old age. My feet and my hip hurt," he cursed, walking into the house.

An uncouth, skinny boy, with beady eyes, perhaps sixteen or seventeen years old, followed him. A glum smile played at the corners of his mouth.

"My grandson, Nikolai, don't be afraid of him. He is a bit loutish, but he is very kind. You should move closer to the table. By the way, my name is Peter Ivanovich."

He busied himself in the kitchen, preparing food for them. Finally, oil sputtered in a pan, and the smell of fried eggs made their stomachs feel queasy.

"Help yourself, dear guests."

Peter Ivanovich fussed around the table, carefully setting down plates for each of them. Then, their generous host deftly heaped theirs plates with eggs, smoked fish and bread. The young soldiers gulped down the food until there was nothing left, and their eyes were heavy with fatigue. The old man himself joined them at the table, slurping up his food ravenously, with obvious pleasure.

"How did it happen that you lost your comrades?" Peter Ivanovich asked them between mouthfuls of hot food, still watching their every movement.

"We were surrounded by German soldiers, and only a few of us managed miraculously to break through the enemy lines and to escape unscathed. We groped through the woods for three days until we reached your village."

"What battalion did you belong to?" He scowled as he spoke but tried to hide his mounting discontent.

They exchanged glances at this unexpected, disquieting question.

"We can't give you that information. In the morning, you should help us find a Russian commander."

Leon, becoming a bit nervous, gave him a long stare. The old man's questions were beginning to sound like an interrogation.

"Then, my dear friends, seek counsel in your pillow. We will talk about it in the morning," he agreed with a hint of dryness, but a barely concealed smile didn't leave his withered face.

A short time later, he turned his attention to the boy who had retreated into silence during their conversation.

"Go and make beds for our guests and hurry up, it's getting late."

The boy obediently got up to prepare a sleeping place on the floor in the next room.

"Sleep well," the old man said to all of them and glanced, smiling sweetly.

In spite of their fatigue, they couldn't fall asleep for some time. They left the window flung wide open. The dead of night encroached on the unknown town. A light wind began to blow more strongly. The small house reverberated with the wind. Frightened, they listened to the first peal of thunder, coming from a distance. Under gusts of wind, the casements shook: then thunder rattled the windowpane, until it fell with a joyful jingle to the floor. They could now hear steady patter of rain, drumming louder against the roof. Soon, the rain stopped, and they sank into a leaden and troubled sleep.

Before daybreak, Peter Ivanovich woke them up. "Wake up, wake up," he shouted, sounding alarmed.

By now, the weather had cleared, and the first pale sunrays peeped into the room. Mark and Leon left the room first so that Rita could get dressed. They washed their faces with cold water, and slowly, they were revived from their heavy slumber. Soon, Rita emerged from the room in a simple cotton dress. Her sleek raven black hair was pulled back into a bun, in a way that accented the perfection of her fine features. Her eyes shone, but there were still red spots on her face. She was running a temperature, and both Mark and Leon noticed her feverish look. She saw the worried glances on Mark's face and with a supple movement pulled him aside.

"What is going to happen to us? I don't trust Peter Ivanovich. Mark, I just don't trust him. He seems to me a fake. Please listen to me. We have to leave this house right away. Don't dally, Mark, please hurry. Trust my intuition," she desperately pleaded with him again and again, her voice dropping to a secretive whisper. He took her hand in his, not knowing what to say. She freed her hand.

"Whatever happens to us, remember that I'll love you as long as I live." She looked at him questioningly. He heard vehemence in her voice.

"We will be always together, Rita. Don't think about death. The war will end soon. I believe. We will get married and have a son. We will name him Alexander. In Greek it means a 'defender of men'"

She tried to smile at him, but her lips wouldn't obey. She felt suddenly faint, and her heart began to palpitate.

"Yes, we will name our son Alexander," she announced, giving him a fleeting kiss. "Mark, could you please keep my pregnancy a secret? I feel somewhat ashamed. We are not yet married. Please, do not tell Leon. Promise?"

"Sure, I promise, darling. You have nothing to worry about. I know how to keep secrets."

He touched her belly and smiled.

"I hope it will be a son."

"I want a daughter, Mark."

"Well, the next one will be a girl, but you should take care of yourself, darling. I am so worried about you."

She was no longer listening to him. "We have to go, Mark, they are waiting for us, and I am so hungry."

Rita untied the ribbon that held her luxuriant hair and let it swoop freely down.

"You will look beautiful in a white wedding dress," he said dreamily, adoring her beauty and caressingly her hair with his hand.

When they came into the kitchen, breakfast was already waiting for them. A hot samovar puffed in the middle of the table. Somewhere, they heard gunshots and the frightening cries of birds.

"Look," Leon turned to Rita, "we have just talked it over, and we think that you should stay here for a while. You need time to recover while we will conduct some reconnaissance to try to find out how far away the Nazis are."

"I'll go with you," Rita feverishly objected because deep down she trembled for their lives.

"God forbid that anything should happen. You'd better stay with us, young girl. Let them do their work. You should help me around the house," the old man put in emphatically, "We need a woman around here. I'll give you new clothes, nobody will suspect anything."

He took her overcoat and her boots.

"Forget about your fancy-schmancy outfit. I'll burn it. You look much better in this flowery dress that belonged to my daughter."

"By the way, do you have any documents?" he suddenly inquired and looked questioningly at Mark and Leon.

This question threw them into confusion. "No, we have none. We buried them in the woods."

"Very well, we will try to figure out how to provide you with new fake documents by the time you return." He stared at both of them intently.

Leon brooded over the situation for some time and then

asked the old man if he had a map.

"No, I don't have a map, but I'll show you the way out of the village. You should really hurry up. I'll send my grandson to accompany you half the way. As I told you before, the Nazis can't be far from here. If they find you in the house, they won't spare our lives. I suspect that you twins are Jews. Are you not?" He glared at Mark and Leon, carefully examining their faces. The old man seemed to be very upset.

"Does it make any difference?" Leon was astonished by this question.

"Yes, it does. Don't try to evade my question. If they find out that you stayed in my house, they'll kill my grandson and me. And I mean not just the Nazis...but members of the guerrilla squad." The tone of his voice was unexpectedly harsh.

He interrupted his sentence and cocked his ear to hear what might be going on outside. Then, Peter Ivanovich brought a piece of paper and a pencil to draw a small map. He pulled his chair up next to Leon. Leon peered over his shoulder, watching how the old man drew his simple map.

"The wooded area starts right behind the street. In order to avoid danger, try to get deeper into the woods and move in the direction of the sunrise. Soon, you'll notice an old windmill. It's about here," he said, pointing to the map. "The man, who lives there, would be able to help you. He'll show you the best way to evade the Nazis and how to find our soldiers. Go now, I hope to see you again....Don't worry about the girl. I won't hurt her. I promise you, you can trust me. I am an old lonely man, and the girl can give me a hand and help out about the place," he said, grinning and showing his broken yellow teeth.

Mark rose decisively from his chair and walked towards Rita.

"Don't cry, Rita. I'll see you in an hour or so. You should stay here. It is safer in your condition," he said with gritty determination.

He tried to dispel her apprehensions, all the while struggling to hide his feelings and to appear strong. Yet his eyes betrayed his emotion when he tenderly embraced Rita.

Leon took the map out of the man's hands. "We'll go now."

"Wait just a minute," Peter Ivanovich said as he peered out the window.

Not seeing anything suspicious, he shuffled outside. From the steps of his house he could see the street all the way down to the end. Under the morning sun, it looked as if it were painted with pale watercolors. He stood there for some time, listening to the morning sounds and carefully inspecting the empty street. A strong autumn fragrance passed through the open door into the house.

"I think that you can go now," he muttered, taking a deep breath, "and, please, be careful. However, discretion is the better part of valor. God bless you all."

He was holding the door wide open, signaling to them that it was now safe to leave the house.

"Please, take good care of Rita," Mark urged and looked beseechingly at Peter Ivanovich, Never before in his short life had he known such a moment of somber presentiment and grief.

The man blessed them and crossed himself three times. His eyes became moist as he resumed confidently, "You have nothing to worry about, young man. It's time to hoist sail. Godspeed."

At the doorway, Mark made a quick move and looked back at Rita one more time. He lingered and waited for a second, as if he wanted to tell her something very important, but she understood him without words. Her pallid face and her eyes full of fear made him suddenly aware of the danger. His heart sank at the idea he might never see her again. She wanted to follow him, but understanding she would only be a burden, remained motionless. How could he know that soon after his disappearance Rita, fearing for her life and not trusting the old man anymore, had to leave the house in search of a safer place to stay?

Leon stood aside, stealthily watching Rita. His sorrowful heart yearned for her love. Caught up in the sadness of parting with Mark, she had forgotten about Leon who had never had a chance to reveal to Rita his deep feelings for her. Finally, they thanked the old man for his hospitality and stepped outside, cautiously closing the door behind them, the door that was about to separate them forever from the woman they both so deeply loved.

Chapter Twenty-Five
The Captivity

*T*hrough the naked trees the autumn sun looked pallid and cold. The languid, autumn sunlight didn't spill any warmth over the earth. The cold sun came to a standstill, as if waiting for something to happen. The shriveled leaves rustled under their feet. The tall trees, like devoted soldiers, bent their heads, watching their every step. As they moved stealthily between the mute trees, the unusual quietude of the early morning scared them.

Nikolai accompanied Mark and Leon all the way to the windmill without a word. They walked out of the woods and forged ahead through a small shrubby thicket. And it was only at the end of their journey that Nikolai whined a few words to them, wishing them luck before he ducked haltingly back into the woods. They lay doggo, lurking behind a clump of bushes, hiding in the dark shade of the tufted branches. Meanwhile, they carefully inspected this unfamiliar place. The morning dew crawled under their clothes and friendly licked their faces. They were waiting for something, delaying their next move.

In truth, they were too worn out after so many months of pitched battles, so much uncertainty. Their young hearts were already full of sorrow and grief—they had seen so much: death, murder, destruction. They couldn't accept the savagery of war and the unspeakable horror of death. During this short time of war, their lives had turned out to be so different from their dreams—instead of love, they found hate; instead of boyhood and adventures, they saw a real war. They learned how to hate and how to kill. What fate awaited them? Was it a road to nothingness, to nowhere?

Mark noticed a small motionless sparrow on the ground near his foot, snuggled down under a pile of leaves, and picked him up. The dead bird was covered with dirty fluff. A sudden pity for this tiny defenseless creature pierced his heart. He squeezed Leon's hand and showed him the dead bird. It looked as if it had been attacked by a vicious dog. Leon covered the sparrow with leaves, and they dug a small hole to bury it. Only then, in the lee of bushes, they began their stealthy advance, trying to keep their eyes on the windmill, when suddenly they heard a strange sound, as if the wind were bending the tops of the trees. They pricked up their ears, but it was too late. Then...something dreadful and unexpected happened.

The morning suddenly came to life: the trees were shaking, a dog was barking, then—gunshots and more gunshots. The hysterical scream of a German officer made them jump.

"Hands up! Hands up!"

They stood for a second with their hands raised in defeat, trying to figure out what to do next, and how many officers were hiding behind the bushes. However, at that very moment, they felt something horrific, shaggy and strong pounce on them and knock them down on the ground. They didn't have a chance to push the animals back. As they fell down, they realized that these were malicious hunting dogs that the Germans trained to guard prisoners. The dogs lay on them, pressing their bodies to the ground, breathing heavily into their faces, biting and barking loudly. They latched onto their bodies while two SS officers, like gravediggers, watched the whole scene with cold, glassy eyes. In a couple of minutes, they were outdone by their enemies.

Mark looked up and saw the liquid sun, hiding behind a black cloud. The cloud darted away and the molten sun tipped over him and fell on his chest. It pressed on him heavily, making it impossible to breathe. Blood welled up and streamed out of his wounds. He grasped for air, but the blazing sun came back, and he felt as if his whole body were on fire.

Leon didn't make a single sound. Although he didn't feel any pain, he knew that it was the end. And yet, he desperately, passionately wanted to live. They had just set out on life's road. They had not yet had a chance to experience real life when fate threw them into the fire of war. Leon groaned heavily, making an attempt to get up, but a strong kick to his chest made him fall back. Another blow to his face made him groan with pain again. His strength began to wilt away, and he suddenly felt in his mouth the salty taste of blood. In the darkness, Mark fumbled for Leon's hand and gently squeezed it, letting him know that he had to be brave and not to let the Nazis see his weakness or fear, or agony.

Minutes later, pushed by Germans soldiers, beaten severely, they toiled along the same road that led them to the village. Their muddy boots clattered upon the dirty pebbles. The sounds of barking dogs and of crowing roosters wafted to their ears. Somewhere far off, they heard the quiet whisper of nature, waking up to a new day. And they both thought about Rita. Deep in their hearts, they prayed to God to keep her alive and safe.

Suddenly, the morning sun had stopped sending its rays down to earth. It had disappeared in the sky behind the clouds and no longer lit up the road. The cold wind blew from the north, driving the dense stratum of clouds into darkness. A heavy rain fell upon the earth, washing away their footsteps, as if they had never walked on this earth and had never existed in this world. They had become small particles of the vast universe and invisible slaves of the German nation.

The railroad platform, where the Russian prisoners were brought, was swallowed up in the impending darkness. Twilight, like an ugly beast, had already invaded the village, spreading its black wings over the sky. The local train station, poorly lit, was scarcely visible....The air was full of sounds—the loud shrieks of the German soldiers, sudden gunshots, the barking of dogs, and the noise of the approaching freight train. This train was about to dispatch them to an unknown place for further torture as prisoners of war.

They both noticed that the first car of the train had a sign in German *'Nur für Deutsche.'* (*Germans only*). The last car stopped right across from Mark and Leon and opened its door into pitch darkness. Mark tried to support Leon who could hardly stand on his own after being mercilessly mauled by the vicious dogs. Blood was streaming from his wounds, and his face was covered with blood, but he managed to smile.

"Be brave, Mark, you have to stay alive for Rita, she'll be waiting for you. Your life is now more important than mine," he uttered losing his strength.

Suddenly, they heard scattered raucous shouts as German soldiers in their green uniforms marched towards them and then abruptly stopped. One of the soldiers, with a particularly sinister face, holding a gun in his hand, separated from the other soldiers and took a step forward, closer to Leon, his eyes roving over him. The other soldiers turned around and paraded farther on, to the next line of prisoners.

"Keep quiet," the soldier murmured to Leon in German. He directed a harsh light on Leon's face, examining him as though under a microscope, but then he switched it at Mark, and a look of unexpected pity crossed his worn face. He was thinking at that moment about his own twin brother who had disappeared without a trace somewhere in wintry Russia. He stood for a minute, staring at them, and then, looking cautiously around, stretched out his hand and slipped a piece of bread into Leon's hand. Perhaps, this tiny shred of kindness gave them the courage to survive the hardship of their endless journey into the unknown.

Both brothers were pressed together and squashed between the other prisoners as they were forced into darkness of the fright car. Leon was shivering convulsively, and Mark struggled to hold his body still. Under a dim and almost ominous light from an overhead bulb they silently prayed. They repeated their prayers with other prisoners, hoping that it would help them to forget their pain. They could only guess what lay ahead, and they had no choice but to accept whatever was awaiting them in an unknown land. The railroad platform, the last vision of their motherland, swam back into the night and slowly disappeared from view, turning into a small black speck on the map of their past.

* * * * *

"It is such a sad story. Do you know what happened to them?" Eduardo leaned back and stared pensively at Alex.

"Yes, I heard the whole story from my father. They were both shipped to Dachau, where countless prisoners died, and hundreds were forced to participate in cruel medical experiments. Somehow, Leon managed to stay with his brother, but at the beginning of the winter of 1942, they were separated. Mark was moved along with other prisoners, more than a thousand Russians, to a camp, somewhere in Austria. Unfortunately, Leon found out all of this much later when he was searching for his brother's whereabouts.

"You said 'Austria'? How strange it is." Eduardo face paled. "Do you know when Dachau was liberated? Did Leon find what happened to Mark?"

"Yes, Eduardo, I will share with you all I know. On April 29, 1945, the U. S. Army entered Munich and liberated Dachau. When finally American soldiers reached the inner compound of the camp, where the prisoners were held, they could hardly move. In fact, Leon was very ill and spent months in the American hospital before he could stand on his feet again. At that time, he had a chance to go to America, but his dream was to be reunited with his family, his parents and his sister Rebecca, and to find his twin brother, Mark."

"You said that he was looking for Mark. Did he learn anything about his fate?"

"No, not really. Leon stayed in Munich for some time, looking for Mark and trying to decide what to do next. He was too young, too inexperienced in life, and all alone in a foreign land. When the war ended, one of Stalin's postwar plans was to repress the millions of Soviet citizens who were living outside the Soviet Union. Stalin demanded that those "traitors" be sent back to Russia. Upon their return, they were shipped off to forced-labor camps, as bad as the Nazi camps had been during the war. More than fifty percent of Russian citizens, who went to those camps, never came back. It was a terrible time for those who had lost their motherland and had no future to look forward to.

"Yes, I heard about Stalin's madness, Alex. It was such a sad time for those who were waiting for their loved ones." Eduardo gulped a glass of water. "Sorry for interrupting. Please continue."

"It is really sad what Stalin has done to the former prisoners of war. Following his orders, Russian officials tried to convince them to return to their motherland. Like many others, Leon too yielded to their propaganda, believing that he would be free to reunite with his family. He had heard so many stories about people who had returned and finally ended up in Soviet camps. And yet nothing could stop Leon from going back to his parents. He was young and full of hope."

"Alex, did Leon return to Russia?"

"Yes, Eduardo, he did. Upon his arrival in the Soviet Union, Leon was taken straight from the train to a forced-labor camp in Siberia. It was his misfortunate fate to go from a Nazi camp to a Soviet one.

After Stalin's death, in 1953, Leon was released from the camp. On his way home, he met a Polish girl, Agnes, from the same camp who, like him, was wandering around the country without any money or anyone to help her. Leon managed to find odd jobs, supporting himself and Agnes. Soon afterwards, he returned home to Nevel with his new wife."

Chapter Twenty-Six
Portrait in an Oval Frame

*A*lex cleared his throat and continued, "By this time, the boy, Alex, had grown up and was a pretty clever thing, full of life and energy, spoiled by his grandparents. Leon learned from his mother the tragic fate of this boy and treated him as if he were his own son. One day, Eliza showed him a picture in an oval frame of the woman who had given birth to the child. Leon took the portrait and looked at it for a longtime. Watching him, his mother realized that the photograph awakened in him some mystery from his past, unlocked some deep pain that had been hidden in his heart for a long time.

Leon could not take his eyes off the woman's face. At last, he muttered, "I knew her well. She was a nurse in our battalion. Mark and I, we were both in love with her, but she fell in love with Mark. He hoped to find her one day and get married. Her name is Rita."

A stunned silence fell over the room.

"Then, whose child is this?" Eliza asked confusingly.

"I don't really know. It could be Mark's child."

His grandmother cried. Many painful memories came rushing back to her. After discussing it for many days, they finally decided to tell the boy that Leon was his real father.

Even after Stalin's death, his legacy lived on for some time. Leon's parents begged him to find a way to leave the

175

country. Meanwhile, Agnes continued to look for her relatives in Poland. One day, she received an invitation to visit them.

"So, eventually, Leon left Russia. Did he ever see his parents again?

"Be patient, Eduardo, my story is coming to the end. From Poland Leon with Alex and Agnes went to America. A short time later, after they had settled in New York, Agnes died of pneumonia. She had suffered too much for too long, and her health was totally destroyed by the hard labor in the Soviet zone. Well, apparently Leon had to move on with his life—there was Alex, his son.

Leon had always carried with him the portrait of a beautiful woman in an oval frame. One day, he had revealed to Alex the truth about his parents and asked him to cherish this photo of the young woman, who was his real mother. As for his parents, Leon has never seen them again."

* * * * *

Alex looked at Eduardo who at the moment was trying to recapture his own past. Alex opened his briefcase and produced a small photograph in an oval frame of a woman with a lovely face, beautifully shaped by luxuriant black hair.

"Is this her?" Eduardo stared at the portrait.

"Yes, this is my mother."

Eduardo's face froze in disbelief.

"Yes, I believe this picture is of my mother," Alex repeated, watching how Eduardo too opened his briefcase and took out a small drawing of a woman in an oval frame. To Alex's disbelief, it was a well-executed drawing of the same woman, Alex's mother.

"So, if this woman is your mother too, you are my half-brother."

Eduardo put the drawing back into his briefcase, watching with pleasure the shock on Alex's face.

"Alex, let me understand—Leon suspected that Mark was

your real father?"

"Yes, but I do not understand, I am really confused...." Alex murmured, staring at him incredulously.

"Actually, Alex, now, it is my turn to tell you my story. My father was also a Russian, and he was also a prisoner of a Nazi concentration camp....Here is the story....The grass was wet and cold, but the ground was soft, almost like a fluffy bed he had been dreaming about for all those years...."

Chapter Twenty-Seven
Man without a Past

*T*he grass was wet and cold, but the ground was soft, almost like a fluffy bed he had been dreaming about for all those years. There was a fresh scent of earth as it usually happens after a rainy day. The familiar scent brought back a half-forgotten memory.

He moved his arms and found himself prostrate on the ground in an odd position—face down, like a wounded bird with broken wings. Mark made an attempt to get up, to raise himself from the ground, but an excruciating pain in both legs made him fall back. He tried to scream, but the scream was weak, not much more than a whisper. Its echo died somewhere behind the mountains. He licked his lips which were parched with thirst. Mark touched the wet grass and then pressed his hand against his lips and forehead. The cold moisture penetrated his burning skin and brought him some relief.

The morning sun was just beginning to shine. The first warm sunlight touched his aching body, but his consciousness was still hovering in space between night and dawn. Finally, Mark lifted his head and looked around. A stunningly beautiful view unfolded before his eyes. He saw mountains of imposing beauty, flanking him on both sides. They seemed to be so very close to him that he even imagined he could touch their cold stones. The mountains didn't blend into the background but looked like his guards, standing there to protect him from the bitter wind. He saw the sky, blazing with clear blue and pink shades, turning almost lilac in the far distance. The sun was rising from above the mountains. Their apexes shone under the rays of sun.

All this beauty, painted by the mysterious colors of nature, took his breath away. He hardly noticed how badly he had been shivering from the cold air penetrating his sodden, threadbare clothes. *Was he no longer being held? Was he now out of the danger that had followed his every step? But how could that be?* These thoughts goaded him to action. Mark made another attempt to turn over, and this time he was successful. He lay on his back, staring into the cloudless sky. He tried now to put his thoughts in order, but in vain— his memory was shattered. His tired brain refused to obey him and to connect him with his past. Only a few foggy shreds that he could not quite grasp emerged from his burning mind. Entranced by the peaceful scenery, Mark inhaled the cold misty air deep into his lungs and then, groaning with pain, fell into oblivion.

* * * * *

Mark opened his eyes again, still struggling to understand where he was, but could discern nothing. Night had suddenly fallen on earth. The darkness was so intense that his eyes could not penetrate it. All he could see was the black menacing moon, oozing out through the open window, and the black, scarcely visible silhouettes of the mountains, staring at him through the heavy clouds. He saw the big monstrous shadow of a bird with spread wings, crawling slowly on the opposite wall. But there was no bird—there was only the silence of the night. The midnight quietude scared him for a moment.

He tried to hoist himself to his feet, but again the pain in both legs forced him to fall back on the pillow. *Pillow? Soft and fluffy pillow? How could it be?* He touched it, realizing that he was resting on a real bed. A sudden feeling of liberation filled his whole being. Mark let out a cry, still very weak, hardly audible, light as a feather, which flew away into the unknown space. The shadow on the opposite wall disappeared as if scared of his sudden cry. At first, he could think of nothing at all, petrified by silence and the frightening black moon, staring at him through the thick wall of the dark. He thought that the moon was black probably because it was begrimed with dust from the ashes of those who had perished in crematoriums. Their eyes stared at him from beyond, from a remote place of his consciousness where his previous life and his memory had been taken away from him.

He repeated loudly the word 'crematorium', and suddenly whole images from the recent past came rushing back to him as if painted in inky, dirty colors on a gigantic canvas. He was frightened by sudden flashes of memory that had no beginning, no end, but only those last hours of his life, illuminated by this black moon....He saw emaciated faces, wasted bodies and eyes crying for help. He saw vividly now the iron fences, the barracks....

And then, in a lightning flash, for an instant, memories came rushing back to him. He saw the Nazis, bustling with panic, packing and loading their trucks in a frantic hurry. Late at night, under the same black, starless sky, they loaded as many prisoners as they could into open trucks. The heavy-laden vans took the direction that was familiar to every prisoner—they were headed to their last destination, to the end of their lives—the gas chambers. He was the last one to be thrown into the open van. He looked up and saw at the edge of the sky a tiny star, blazing somewhere beyond the visible arch of the horizon, this familiar star, struggling to survive on the border between life and death.

"Soon," he thought, *"I too will turn into a small lonely particle of the sky, or an echo, lost somewhere in the moun-*

tains." It was maddening to think that the end was so near, so tangible, perhaps just around the corner. The truck suddenly made a sharp turn, and Mark felt how friendly hands pushed him out of the fast-moving vehicle. And then...the vision escaped him.

The night was still so desperately quiet. He was surrounded by a dark space, not really knowing where he was and if he was alive. And yet he felt being somehow connected with this unknown space, with this black moon and smoky mountains, flashing on the horizon. A flame was rapidly growing inside him, filling up his body, his lungs and then, spreading all over the room—everything was on fire—smoke everywhere, as if he were dying with his friends in the Nazis' gas chamber.

Having difficulty breathing, Mark began to lose consciousness. He made another attempt to lift his head, but hallucinations seized his brain, and he couldn't distinguish anymore between his delirium and reality. Shadow after shadow swam through his burning mind—shadows of the dead—familiar and unknown faces, vanishing somewhere behind the mountains, back to their unreal world, and among them he saw his own shadowy silhouette. Time, space and memory—all intertwined and froze in this strange, dark, intangible world, illuminated only by a black moon.

* * * * *

He was sunk into a deep sleep for some time—sleep, full of troubled dreams. He woke when the first ray of sunlight peeped through the window, sending a shaft of light onto his face. He dozed for some time, totally unaware of his whereabouts until he heard a sort of rustle, perhaps a puff of wind and then, in the aperture of the door, he saw a silhouette of a woman, emerging from the sunlight. She had a kind and winsome face. He lifted his hand and stretched it out to touch her, to make sure that she was real, but there was an abyss between them, a black hole of space with only some flashes of sunlight, coming through the open window.

He then felt the gentle touch of a hand on his forehead and the tender, soft, voice of a woman, *"Siete dal pericolo. Sarete sicuro con me qui. Gli ho portato un certo alimento.*[6]*"*

He understood her because he had learned Italian in the camp from his Italian comrade.

As the shroud of mist had risen, he saw a tray with a coffeepot, a bowl with porridge and a piece of bread with cheese. He had long forgotten the taste of real food and the voice of a real woman. Mark smiled at her as for the second time in his short life he experienced the miracle of coming back from the dead.

* * * * *

"Please finish your food. You have to get your strength back to keep alive. It looks as if both your legs are broken, but I am a nurse, and I can help you."

She talked without turning on the light, afraid to scare him. The sunlight was still glowing between their pale faces. He began eating his porridge while the woman gently held his head above the pillow.

"I appreciate your help, but I can't accept your kindness. I know that by hiding me here you will jeopardize your own life. I really have to go."

Mark made another attempt to get up but winced in pain when the woman pushed him gently back on the pillow.

"Don't even try to escape. The Germans have left, and there is no danger for us anymore. You are too weak, and you need rest."

She took the empty plate and moved closer a cup of hot coffee which sent out a delicious aroma, a scent of something familiar and yet long forgotten.

"This will give you some strength. You have to eat, really. It is such a miracle that you are alive."

---

[6] You are out of danger. You'll be safe with me here. I brought you some food.

The smell of coffee made him feel giddy. He couldn't understand everything she was saying to him, but the timbre of her voice was tender, her hands were soft and her lovely face—kind.

"Qual è il tuo nome?" [7] he asked her in his broken Italian.

"Francesca is my name, Francesca Mancini. I am Italian. What about you?"

"I am Marco." He made a long pause, trying to remember something, and then with some hesitation added, "Goldano, yes, Marco Goldano. That's how my Italian friend called me—Marco Goldano. I don't remember where I came from and where I was born. I don't know what happened to me before I found myself in that concentration camp."

"You probably have amnesia. Don't worry, I am sure it will pass with time. It happens sometimes. You were a prisoner of Mauthausen, a concentration camp. I found you unconscious near the road. You have nothing to fear. I know—it will make you feel better to find out that the war is over. I think that under the conditions you have endured, the loss of memory is normal. I am sure it'll come back, but now you have to rest. You probably have family somewhere, and they are waiting for your return. You have to live for them. Don't you want to live after everything that you went through?"

His eyes slowly closed. He was still too weak to talk with Francesca. She hesitated for a moment and then bent over and gave him a fleeting kiss on the cheek. Mark felt the warmth emanating from her body, her soft lips on his cheek, and he fell into a state of fleeting tranquility. In his half-sleep, somewhere far away, he heard the first loud church bells ringing, and then the others chiming in. It was such familiar music from his distant, all-but-forgotten childhood.

---

[7] Qual è il tuo nome? (Italian) What is your name?

Chapter Twenty-Eight
Flashbacks

A few weeks passed, and Mark found out the place where he was now living was called Mattighofen. It was a lovely town in Austria, situated at the edge of a little hill, stretching down to the Matting River and the romantic Schwemmbach Brook. They lived far from the hustle and bustle of busy city life, in a tiny, crude cottage, surrounded by the beauty of nature—forests and high plateaus, lakes and meadows.

As the days went by, Mark's health began to improve. His young body fought to live. Every day, Francesca was by his side, caring, trying to alleviate his pain, physical and emotional. She was delighted to have Marco with her and to care for him, and watch how rapidly his conditions improved. She was happy, when leaning on her shoulder, he squeezed her hand in his, carefully taking his first steps in her tiny, cozy house. She guided him when they walked outside on the warm sunny days and the quiet moonlit nights. They often admired together the beauty of the scenery. Sometimes, they sat outside under an old, oak tree with wide branches, enjoying the warm weather or reading her favorite books.

Francesca began to teach Marco Italian and was impressed by his ability to learn the language—he turned out to be an ardent student, always eager to learn. Francesca would bring him books from the library. While she was at work, he spent most of his time reading. They were now all alone in the whole world—two lonely souls with a tragic past and uncertain future, two souls desperately searching for happiness.

Everything around him—the peaceful scenery, the warm breezes and the light scent of flowers, intoxicated him, made him forget his past. However, with time, Francesca began noticing that he often languished into obscurity, wanting to be left alone, ignoring her presence. She wondered if his soul was slowly drifting away from her, away from the real world, where he had now existed and was constantly searching for his forgotten years. Although with his continuing recovery, he showed some good signs of gaining strength, he was still deeply troubled by the profound loss of memory of his distant life. He still had those black holes in his mind. He could not find his way around, no matter how hard he struggled to remember his childhood, his parents and the place of birth. He tried to forget those miserable days in the concentration camp, when death followed his every movement, casting a dark shadow of terror on his tormented soul. Terror? How many years had he lived in this constant state? Only now, he began to free himself from its monstrous fetters and to breathe freely without looking back in fear that his every step was being watched.

There were times, when in the sleepless hours of the night, flashbacks would come to haunt him. He saw an old synagogue, facing a picturesque lake, old oaks and weeping willows, bowing low over the dead water, surrounding its old walls. At times, he would suffer from hallucination, and he saw himself sauntering along the river with a young man who looked like his mirror reflection. Sometimes, he felt as if he were dwelling in a different dimension—unfamiliar faces, strange rigid landscapes, a dark lake and an old cemetery with a lacey wooden fence. These fleeting images appeared in his sick mind and then vanished into the unknown.

As for Francesca, she was profoundly religious. She saw a sign from God in Marco's appearance in her life. He now belonged to her, and only to her. Her goal was to make him happy by helping him forget his past. Deep in her heart, she feared the return of his memory. She was afraid of losing him. However, with time their attachment to each other grew deeper by the day as did his total dependence on Francesca.

One day, he asked her for a piece of paper, pencil and oil paints. In amazement, she watched him drawing her portrait.

"You are so beautiful, Francesca. Your dark hair and blue eyes are in such contrast with your complexion. It is such a pleasure to paint your expressive face. We don't even know each other, and yet I feel at home with you, the home I probably had, but don't remember it any longer."

"I heard you speaking Polish or Russian in your sleep, but you look Italian. You are a very handsome man, Marco. My husband too was a handsome man. He was a German soldier, and he was killed at the very beginning of the war, somewhere in Poland. Perhaps, it is for the best. He was too young and too naïve to understand the horror of this war. He was a good man who was brainwashed. He couldn't hurt a fly."

"Does it still causes you pain?"

Mark put his brush aside to look closely at Francesca and for the first time he saw pain crossing her lovely face. With feverish strokes, he returned to painting her portrait. It was like a miracle being born on the canvas as Francesca's grieving face came to life under his brush.

"You are a genius, Marco. Why didn't you tell me that you are an artist, not just an ordinary artist, but a great one?"

"I didn't know it myself. It is a discovery to me as well."

He peered at the portrait, trying to recollect something long forgotten. He had never complained to Francesca about how many times he had hoped to retrieve his memory, but it kept floating off into oblivion. It felt as if a thick wall had sprung up and didn't allow him to look beyond it. All his attempts to get a glimpse of his past sank into the darkness of obscurity, into the unknown. His memory seemed to have vanished forever, and all he had was his present and perhaps his future. He watched his life from the outside, like a stranger watching the life of a neighbor. And only sometimes, varied reminiscences would recapture the familiar aroma of grass or flower. He would wake up every morning with the resolve—from that day on he would begin building a new world, he would make Francesca happy—but how little it meant to him, his future, when he still had no memory and no past.

Chapter Twenty-Nine
Mysterious Drawings

*M*ark was tall, with curly dark hair, soft skin and delicate hands. He had exquisite and graceful manners. Francesca was impressed. But his shy, gentle smile was rarely seen. Most of the time, his grieving eyes were looking inward, into soul. He was a strange man, reserved and distant from the rest of the world. Yet, when he painted, his strong slanted brush stokes reflected his fiery temperament and flamboyant emotions.

Watching him paint, Francesca often ruminated over his artistic talent and his creative energy. He worked with obsessive inspiration and powerful determination. His eyes burned with passion, his lips twisted, and his face had an almost unearthly expression. His paintings had opened the door to an unreal world, away from the bitterness of the outside world. At first glance, the rage of colors blinded and disturbed Francesca, but then there was magic—she would become magnetized by his unusual and powerful palette of colors. The same magic happened in her heart and her soul, and she surrendered to the power of her emotions.

One early morning, when Francesca had left for work, Marco experienced a strange feeling, as if his brain had suddenly been set on fire. With trembling hands he grabbed a brush. Mysteriously, the face of another woman began slowly to crystallize in his imagination. Then, in a dream-like state, he painted another portrait of that imaginary, unknown woman holding a child, until finally, her features sailed away from him, and he fell into delirium. The daylight swam into twilight, but Mark didn't wake up. He had some strange dreams. His sleep was peaceful, as if he had been drained of all his strength and had exhausted all his emotions.

When Francesca returned home from work, she found Marco sleeping peacefully behind the house. He had fallen asleep in front of the isle with his head drooped down on his chest and a brush in his hand. The warm wind blew his curly hair, and the last dying sunrays fell on his face, calm in his dream, almost happy. Francesca stood there, frozen in place, watching Marco's face in his sleep, realizing how far away from her he was in that instant.

She watched closely when Marco opened his eyes and mumbled something under his breath as if talking to himself. She glanced down and took from his hands a brush and a drawing of a girl with refined features, framed by dark, luxuriant hair. The face of the unknown girl mesmerized Francesca with its spiritual beauty. It expressed such depth and such sadness. In the background, a dark forest merged with a dark sky. A black moon was looking down at her as a symbol of love and death. She felt as if Marc and this unknown girl were connected and just moments apart from each other. The portrait suddenly opened the door to his past, revealed to her the whole story, a thousand details of Marco's tragic and forgotten life. The strong brush strokes in the background and the tender colors of the girl's face emerged from the drawing to tell her about the true power of love.

The next drawing fell to the ground. Francesca picked it up and was stunned to see a portrait of the Madonna and Child—the face of the Madonna was the same face as that of the woman. *Did Marco have a child?* Francesca's thoughts were in turmoil. She was distressed not knowing what to do next, unsure of their future. This sudden revelation had cast a shadow over it.

How could she now imagine her life without Marco? He still slept and did not move when she took the drawings out of his hands. It was obvious that he was still living in his dreams, desperately looking for a way to his lost past. Francesca knew that when he woke, he would not remember either the drawings or the face of the woman he had once loved. She went to the house and hid both paintings in a secret place. She couldn't risk her happiness. Francesca decided not to tell him anything until his memory began to show signs of recovery. In the meantime, Mark shouldn't know anything about the girl from his past. When Mark eventually came into the house, Francesca was already bustling around the kitchen preparing dinner. He felt guilty and grateful at the same time.

"I am sorry, darling, I should have prepared dinner myself before you got home, but I fell asleep and lost track of time."

"Did you have a nice dream, Marco?" She looked inquiringly, straight into his eyes, afraid to hear his answer, but what she heard put her mind at rest.

"I don't remember, darling. I don't remember anything, even the dreams I have just had."

"Stop worrying, Marco," she smiled at him, "I don't remember my dreams either. Nobody does. They always disappear the minute you wake up."

"It happens to me in real life, Francesca. The minute I open my eyes in the morning, I can't remember my past, as if I have never lived before this moment."

Mark realized how fortunate he was to be alive and to have Francesca by his side. He felt as if he were being reborn. Little by little, out of darkness and tragedy, out of havoc and pain, a greater love branded deep into their lonely hearts. When it seemed everything inside and outside them had been destroyed, out of ashes, pain and suffering, a new strong feeling had emerged.

The power of love and the fire of creativity moved Mark's brush and his talent flourished. The fame of this great artist had grown among the locals and spread far beyond. Francesca could sell his paintings, and in addition to her work in a hospital, they could live comfortably without thinking of tomorrow.

Strangely enough, Mark neither tried to recreate the painting of a young woman, nor did he remember anything about those two small drawings. Nevertheless, he was often mystified by his own imaginative paintings. He felt they had been brought back from his remote memory. Once, painting his self-portrait, he painted the same face next to himself, as if he were seeing himself in a mirror. Upon finishing this portrait, he had the feeling that half of his heart and soul had been lost somewhere in another remote space. This staggering discovery made him wonder more often about his life before he found himself in the Austrian concentration camp. However, he was growing used to his new environment, to Francesca, to this small, cozy house and the mesmerizing beauty of the Alps that had inspired him so greatly.

In less than a year, Marco and Francesca got married. By this time, Francesca was carrying his child. After all his suffering, life had granted them happiness. His life was now a seamless procession of days devoted to his work and peaceful evenings with his wife.

As for Francesca, her worries about Marco's past memories dissolved in their happy time together. She desperately wanted to believe that their happy live would never end. However, in one tragic moment everything collapsed, and their happiness fell apart like a house of cards.

It happened on the day their son was born. Holding his child in his arms, Marco was lost in a reverie. Even the birth of his baby didn't bring complete solace to his heart as if he were afraid to lose him, afraid that someone would try to take his baby away from him. Somewhere, deep down inside there was still fear. Maybe, it was the same feeling of terror he had experienced before? He realized that this feeling had grown in his heart along with his happy days as something forgotten, like the vision of a small lonely star he always saw beyond the horizon during his sleepless nights, the remote, resplendent star of his dream.

It was almost midnight when Marco returned home from the hospital. He was happy—in a week he would bring home his wife and their newborn son whom they had named Eduardo. He went outside to search for his lucky star, to share with her his happiness, but the star was not there. Instead, a huge dark cloud, moving from behind the mountains, dappled the sky and turned the moon again into a black sphere. The air was full of sounds, and the scent of mountain blossom filled the air. Dream-like memories of something familiar fluttered up in his mind.

Looking into the pitch darkness, as if awakening from a long dream, his eyes began to behold a different picture. His memory surged and receded like strong ocean waves. Time floated back, turning into a familiar road that led him out of darkness. Slowly, he began to hallucinate, revisiting a small island of his memory, forgotten long ago and locked away from the rest of the world—the island of his past. His mind conjured up a picture of the flowing water of a river and the lusterless surface of a lake, a small cemetery with a wooden lacey fence. Like an old imaginative painting, far away he saw a house at the turn of a river, near a cemetery, and a dark river, flowing into a picturesque lake. There was a red cloud of smoke, rising above the water.

Happy memories crowded in on him as his eyes traveled farther down the river. He saw himself walking with his twin brother along the bank. It was the day when their peaceful lives had suddenly ended. Step by step, he summoned up their last summer together. The grass, thick, dark-green, had grown up into the sky, piercing it with its sharp ends, trying to break off the morning dust and eventually disappearing in the evaporating clouds. The rising sun emerged from behind the trees, and sunrays fell upon the earth. He could hear the loud shriek of seagulls, flying away and then coming back to the water.

And then slowly, his memory began to recover all the details of his life—his parents, Rebecca, Leon, the happy days with his family. Now, he remembered the day when war broke out and then....Mark succumbed to those familiar images that were slowly materializing from his forgotten life. He felt a sharp stab of pain....

Rita, Rita, he whispered into the night. It was the name of the woman he loved, the woman who had carried his child.

While wandering into his past, Mark forgot the present and didn't care about his future anymore—he returned to his youth to relive it again with all its happy times and all the tragedy, and most of all his deep love for the girl with the luxuriant, black hair. After agonizing hours of retrieving his past, he knew he would not be able to continue living in the present. Marco took a piece of paper and began writing a letter:

My dear Francesca, my love,

Walking back from the hospital into an empty house, I realized I can't live without you. You are my love, my angel who brought me back to life. Now, there are the three of us— you, Eduardo and I. It seems I have everything I could ever have dreamed of....But today something happened....I don't know how to describe to you what I experienced when my memory came rushing back to me....The truth is that in my past life I loved a woman who carried my child....

He couldn't finish the letter. Along with his memories, pain had been growing inside his heart like a fire. The flames were powerful enough to burn down the bridge that invisibly connected him with his present life. His wounded soul flew away into the unknown, into the timeless emptiness of the universe. The moon emerged from the darkness and grazed the summit of the mountains. The lonely familiar star appeared high in the clear firmament to illuminate his final journey to eternity and to bid its last farewell. It seemed as for a moment peace and tranquility hung over the earth, and all the despair, the horrors of war, like a breath of evil, turned into ashes. Slowly, the moon became black again, and pitch darkness mantled the mountains. In this dark space, he heard the lamenting and chanting litany for those who had perished forever. He saw their shadows moving into obscurity, leaving behind them their past and their shattered dreams. He saw glowing light shooting from above, and then his heart stopped beating.

Chapter Thirty
Vicissitudes of Fate

"**Y**ou didn't finish your story, Eduardo. What happened next?"

"Next? Well, after my father—or to be more exact, I can firmly conclude now, our father died of a heart attack, my mother went back to Italy to live with her aunt. Francesca could still sell Marco's paintings to make a decent living for both of us. His work was selling well and was soon exhibited in many galleries around the country. One day, when I turned eighteen years old, my mother showed me the two drawings that she had put away and kept hidden for all those years. One drawing was a portrait of the woman in an oval frame. The other one was also of that beautiful girl but with a child, a boy. Mark painted her as Madonna and Child.

"Why did you say our father?" Alex interrupted Eduardo.

"Yes, because I am sure now that Marco was your father too. Why do you think he painted a portrait of your mother with a child and that letter....?"

Suddenly, as if remembering something, Eduardo opened his briefcase and put on the table a photograph of another drawing. It was a well-executed portrait of two young handsome men in their early twenties, who looked like twins.

"It's a self-portrait of our father. It was a mystery to me why he always painted two faces instead of one. Now I understand. Keep all these drawings, and perhaps one day you will be able to trace deeper the mystery of our past. This is the end of my story, Alex," he confessed.

Alex took the portrait of two brothers into his hands and scrutinized it carefully with great curiosity. It was uncanny how much the twins resembled each other and at the same time—both of them.

"This is a portrait of Leon as I remember him when he was young. I assume that the other man is his twin brother, Mark, my real father. What a strange chain of events. How sad it is that Leon didn't live long enough to learn the real fate of his twin brother."

"I think that deep in his heart Leon always knew that Mark was my father. Probably, he didn't want to cause me any pain. He was always the only father I knew and loved."

"Alex, but now, it's perhaps your turn to tell me if you know anything about your mother's fate?" Eduardo broke into the flux of Alex's thoughts.

"Unfortunately, I don't know much. When Leon visited Nevel, he made some attempts to find out what had happened to my mother. After exhausting and frustrating inquiries, finally in Moscow's old archives he found out that after being arrested in Nevel as a German spy, she had been sent to a forced labor camp somewhere in Siberia where she had soon died. After Stalin's death her name was cleared, but for her it was already too late."

With those words Alex glanced at the door where Eleanor had appeared. She saw both of them at the same time and was transfixed, unable to move. Alex immediately got up to greet his wife but suddenly felt that something was very wrong.

"Eleanor, please meet my new friend, Eduardo Goldano, also an artist."

Eduardo swiftly rose from his chair and gently shook her hand, unable to take his eyes off her face. Eleanor stared at him too for a prolonged time, rather uneasily. Then, her eyes traveled from one to the other. Alex, watching them covertly, tried to relieve the tension.

"Just imagine, Eleanor, I met Eduardo by chance. It was a complete fluke that we just happened to be in the same place at the same time. It happened incidentally, and incidentally, as you can see, we look alike, and now we have found out that we are even related."

Alex didn't finish his sentence. He caught a startled expression on Eduardo's face.

"Eduardo...Eduardo..." Eleanor repeated again and again in disbelief, almost whispering, ignoring Alex's long speech.

"Nora...." Eduardo wrapped his arms around his brother's wife, as if he had known her all his life. The light scent of her fragrance brought back memories of the snowy day when he saw Nora for the first time in New York, twenty years ago. He and Eleanor exchanged smiles. Her eyes shone. Alex could almost feel how the attraction like electricity jolted through their bodies.

Alex watched the whole scene, wondering about the connection between the two until he finally grasped the truth. *Love is always the winner,* he thought, trying to comprehend the situation and suppress his jealousy. How odd it was that the past repeated itself—both of them too, like Mark and Leon, loved the same woman.

Alex was not sure if he was dreaming or if everything that had happened during those two days was real. Once more, he turned to Eduardo.

"Eduardo, do you still think it was fate that united all of us today?"

"Fate? Oh, no, to be perfectly frank with you, I don't believe in miracles, but I do believe in the power of love. It was the woman in the portrait in an oval frame who guided us and whose love and courage brought us all together. Don't you think so?" Eduardo glanced fleetingly at Nora.

"There's something queer and truly, deeply disturbing about all of these happenings. It's so unexpected. I feel as if in the darkness I suddenly found a door. I opened it, and there, behind that door, there is light, the light born out of darkness. The truth finally has emerged from the mystery of our past. Well, I am afraid that I have to leave you two alone." Alex voice was calm, and he hardly looked at his wife.

He picked up his briefcase, opened the door and walked out, away from his past, away from his failed marriage. No one spoke. No one ran after him. No one tried to stop him, as if he had just turned into an apparition. He felt no pain of separation from Eleanor, Eduardo, his dreams, his world. He knew he would see them again someday—someday, when he would be able to look straight in their faces and convince himself that he was no longer betraying his artistic gift.

A short while later, he walked along the unfamiliar evening streets of New York with its majestic skyscrapers, piercing the dark moonless sky with only one tiny bright star watching over his every move. He knew that soon a new road would spread up before him, and the different path would open to a new beginning. But for now, he was all alone in the world, with an uncertain reality, wondering about the validity of his life.

His mind split up into strange images of his failed marriage, meaningless art and unknown tomorrows. An unfathomable solitude embraced him like a new friend. He remembered the day he arrived in New York when he walked alone along its dark, empty streets. Now, they swallowed into their yawning abyss one more lost soul, searching for a new meaning in life. He remembered Eduardo's praise of his early paintings, his watercolors, and he realized that his own voyage in the sea of life had just begun.

Alex looked at his pocket watch and hastened his steps. A little later, at the train station, he bought a ticket to Philadelphia and checked the time. It was almost midnight on October 7th, 2003. He still had about fifteen minutes to wait for his train.

On the empty platform somebody called his name, "Mr. Gold, Mr. Goo...old." Alex tuned around and faced a portly little man in an ill-fitting business suit. The thought flickered into his mind that he had met him somewhere before. Then he recognized him—it was the same man who on the day of his arrival in New York had kindly offered him the newspaper with the article about the opening of his exhibition.

"What a nice surprise! How did it go?" the man exclaimed joyfully and bowed slightly, extending his hand for a handshake, as if they were old friends.

"You know, Professor, I was there, at your show, but I could not get to you. You were surrounded by your admirers. I think that your work is magnificent, marvelous! I was so impressed by those photographs of you with world leaders, movie stars. And I have no words to describe the beauty of your portraits. You are a genius, Mr. Gold."

Alex tried to object, but the man paid no attention.

"Mr. Gold, it would be such an honor if you will agree to paint my portrait. I'll pay well, really, really well." Now, he looked at Alex questioningly, waiting for a reply.

"Your portrait?"

Alex hesitated before answering, raking the man from head to toe.

"Ha, ha, ha, do you really want me to paint your portrait? It is such a temptation. I can hardly refuse such a magnifycent offer, but I am afraid you are a bit late. Matter of fact, as of today, I am not painting portraits anymore. However, I am sure you won't have any trouble finding a young and talented artist who will be able to perpetuate your face for the centuries to come. Good luck!"

With those words, Alex waved goodbye and rushed down the platform to catch the train that was about to take him away from his past to a new chapter in the still unwritten tale of his life.